The Dragon Lover an...

by

Michael Samerdyke

Rita,

Thanks for reading
The Dragon Lover.

Mike Samerdyke

Second Edition Copyright © 2019 Michael Samerdyke

To

Rita Oakes

a very good

TNEO friend

and

correspondent

Stories

The Dragon Lover

Summer's End

The Vegas Swingers

The Garden Dwellers

Snoozin' Doozie

A Regular Day – No Peanuts

Snowman

Kiss

A Day for Danny Ford

The Three Pig Princes

Jackie Gingerbread

After You Come Others

Ol' Stoneface Speaks

The Red Lady

The Dragon Lover

The first time I saw her in my dreams, it was as if I were watching a movie on a bad TV set. I couldn't hear anything, and everything looked fuzzy, like the set had a lot of snow.

She sat at a long table at what had to be a medieval feast, wearing a crimson dress with one of those pointed hats that always made me think of a dunce cap. Gorgeous brown hair spilled out from beneath that cone to rest on her shoulders. Her face radiated serenity and confidence, as she looked at the men boorishly eating around her. I could see her thick brown eyebrows arch with pride that she was not like them. It was as if her part of the picture came in clearly, leaving the rest blurry around her.

Then I woke up. 4:45 AM. Alone. Waiting to get up and go to my job. Great.

I lay there and thought about her, excited and sad. Excited because my dreams were never this interesting. Sad because she was only a dream.

An idea came to me. I got up, snapped on the light, and took down my Brothers Hildebrandt Fantasy Calendar. Maybe, I told myself as I thumbed through this year, then last year, then 1986, and then finally my fantasy art books, I had seen her in a painting before.

Halfway through the first art book, however, I did what I always do. I forgot about the women and looked at the dragons.

They fascinate me. Each dragon seems so powerful, so awe-inspiring, so grand. The flaring nostrils, the deadly talons, the striking tail, the dazzling scales – I was mesmerized again.

I'm a sucker for books on dragons. Art books and fiction. Not stories where the dragons are good guys or misunderstood. I want my dragons to be mean, fierce, proud. I want people to tremble at my dragons, not smile.

I know what some shrinks would say: "Dissatisfied with a dead-end job, he takes refuge by identifying with images of power." Yeah, me and everybody else, all those millions of out-of-shape jerks who wear the colors of a winning football team.

Anyway, the dragons so engrossed me that I lost track of time and didn't get to the Gordon Heights Public Library until after opening time. That put me on a collision course with a representative of a kind of dragon I couldn't stand in the least: Mrs. Szigathy.

"You're late, Mr. Dolezal." Her voice almost seemed to hiss from behind her clenched teeth. "I suppose that's something you were permitted in your university, but we plain public servants know the value of punctuality."

"It won't happen again, Mrs. Szigathy," I said as I hurried up the stairs.

"The Reference Desk has been swamped this morning! Swamped!" Her voice followed me up the stairs. There was a tone of satisfaction in it, as if the inconvenience I had caused were a personal triumph for her.

At the Reference Desk, I found nothing more pressing than usual: men looking for Auto Repair guides, women looking for books for their children's research papers. It was all stuff I could handle in my sleep.

If only I were asleep, I thought. Then I could see _her_ again.

Instead, I saw Cindy Malek coming over to my desk to be sweet, as she did every morning. One look at Cindy's body straining her clothing made me realize how much I wanted the woman in my dreams instead.

"Szigathy was really on the warpath," Cindy said.

"It was my own fault," I said, interrupting her to stem a flood of sympathy. "I lost track of the time. There was no car trouble. No traffic jam."

"Well, she shouldn't have yelled at you," Cindy said. "She ought to treat us with more respect."

Us.

Ever since I first walked through the doors of the Gordon Heights library, Cindy had insisted on seeing a connection between us. When she learned I read fantasy, she started reading my favorite fantasy novels and giving me drawings of the characters.

To give her credit, Cindy had a good eye, and I enjoyed seeing her work on my walls. She had done a great portrait of the Gray Mouser for me, a moody study in pencil.

"Would Miss Malek please return to the Milne Room?" Mrs. Szigathy's voice asked over the P. A. One could easily hear the acid in her voice.

Cindy turned beet red behind her enormous glasses and departed.

Mrs. Szigathy did have her uses after all, I laughed.

The rest of the day rolled along with the usual boredom. After closing time, Cindy waited for me outside the library doors, puffing away on a cigarette as usual. For all her efforts to interest me, she never seemed to grasp that her smoking really put me off.

"I haven't drawn anything for you in a while, Ed," she said between puffs as I stepped out of the building. "I just bought a new set of colors, so I can really go crazy on this one. Do you want a Kane or a Red Sonja?"

"A dragon," I said sharply, the memory of my dream coming back to me. "I want a dragon. Colorful, frightening, and evil."

Cindy's eyes widened behind her glasses as she took another puff.

"You certainly know what you want," she said.

The crimson woman in the medieval hall flickered before my eyes.

"Yes, I do," I said.

That evening, I dreamed of her again. I still couldn't hear anything, but my vision was clear this time. She stood in the throne room, and I watched her, utterly riveted, as she shouted, stamped her feet, and gestured. The targets of her wrath were an older man, seated on the throne, and a younger man who stood a few steps below her.

Although there was no facial resemblance, I immediately sensed that the king was her father. Perhaps it was the uninhibited way she acted before him, for the young man, although obviously angry at the goings on, held a tight rein on his emotions and seemed to glance at the older man with some fear.

The king regarded his daughter with sad eyes, but his mouth showed an unyielding firmness, now matter how the princess argued. I felt that although he might sympathize with her, his hands were tied by tradition.

I shifted my attention to the young man, who was, I had to say, ruggedly handsome with a battle-scarred face. He was, I guessed, about the same age as the princess, if not a year or two older, and then I suddenly guessed the meaning of this pantomime argument.

This young man wished to marry my princess, whether she wished it or not.

Realizing this, I now noticed the casual arrogance in his eyes and the general loutishness of his expression. I could remember him from the night before, sitting next to my princess at the feast and shoveling food into his mouth.

No wonder she protested against this pre-determined marriage.

Finally, the king rose to his feet and said something. The princess burst into tears and fled the throne room. My gaze followed her, until I saw something that stopped me dead.

Until that instant, I had assumed I was watching something from history, some event that had happened a handful of centuries ago with all of its protagonists and antagonists long dead.

Yet as my princess fled, she ran past a green-and-yellow dragon's head hanging on the wall like a hunting trophy. Moments later, as the annoying suitor strode confidently from the room, he passed the dragon's head with no notice, as if it were no more remarkable than an old nine-point elk head on a wall in a hunting lodge in our world would be.

Somehow, my dream vision approached the dragon's head, to assure myself of its reality. The dull color of the scales around the beast's nostrils suggested to me that this dragon had been a fire breather. The horn at the end of its snout was chipped and blackened, details that screamed authenticity to me.

Then I woke up.

My heart pounded in my chest. I had seen a world where dragons were real. I leaped out of bed, clapped my hands with glee, and then realized that I could do nothing to convince anyone of the reality of my dream or help my princess, who seemed doomed to marry her father's choice. Hollow, I went back to bed, where sleep eluded me for several hours. When it came at last, I didn't dream once.

I made it to work early the next day, to Mrs. Szigathy's smug approval. The day passed without event until I took my break. Almost immediately after the staff room door closed behind me, Cindy entered, toting her portfolio.

"I want to show you my preliminary sketch," she said, unzipping her portfolio. "I'm really proud of it."

She pulled out a large sheet of paper, a pencil sketch of a crouching dragon hissing and ready to spit fire. She had included a detail that caught my eye: a collar of spiked scales that separated the dragon's head from its throat.

"I like that," I said, tapping the paper.

Cindy smiled. "I was thinking about green for the back and dark red for the belly."

"What's this?"

We turned to see Mrs. Szigathy enter the staff room, cigarette and lighter ready in her hand. She lit up and, puffing smoke more dragonishly than any creation of Cindy's ever could, she stalked around the table to look at the drawing.

Cindy quickly put a cigarette in her mouth and lit up.

"You are talented Miss Malek," Mrs. Szigathy said. "Very talented. But this isn't suitable for the children. Too frightening."

"She didn't draw it for the Milne Room," I said. "She drew it for me."

Mrs. Szigathy's eyebrows arched, and her smoke curled upward.

"Aren't you a little old for dragons, Mr. Dolezal? Or is an interest in childish fantasy the benefit of a college education these days?"

My jaw tightened, and I looked at Cindy.

"Green for the back and dark red for the belly will be just fine."

I returned to my desk, leaving the two of them to blow smoke at each other.

That evening, I was so agitated that although I went to bed, it seemed I would never get to sleep. The memory of Mrs. Szigathy's smugness kept me tossing and turning as I tried to think of some sharp rebuttal.

Finally, before I realized it, I was dreaming of her, my princess. She was running through pools of weak moonlight that spilled between thick trees. A noise irritated me until I realized it was the breaking of branches.

Excitement swelled within me. I was hearing this world. Tonight I would actually hear my princess speak!

She ran to a lone tower, standing shunned on a bleak hillside. At the door, she lifted the huge knocker and let it fall. The groaning of metal and the impact of metal on wood made me jolt. Again and again, she knocked on the door.

Finally, the door opened, and a bald man with an eyepatch looked out. He nodded as if he had expected her, and he stood aside to let her enter.

"You know my plight," she said, when the two of them had reached a chamber filled with guttering candles, well-worn books, and hour glasses. "The king insists on my marrying Sir Blorodir."

"I am very well familiar with your problem, Princess Alice," the one-eyed man said, as he turned over an hour glass. "That you are here shows your desperation, for since childhood you have been told not to see Erldan on pain of death."

Alice drew herself up to her full height.

"I do not want to die, but I feel that if I marry Blorodir, I may as well be dead."

Erldan lit a new candle.

"How do you think I may help you?"

"I know you are the most powerful sorcerer in the land," she said.

Erldan put a book on a shelf and chuckled.

"You have no great love for either my father or Sir Blorodir and would enjoy seeing them humiliated."

"And they would enjoy seeing me killed." The sorcerer glared at her, and Alice shrank back. "I will pick the time and place of my revenge on your father. Not you."

After a breath, Alice stepped closer to him.

"I ask you for no spells against my father or Blorodir. Only give me a champion, someone to help me in my distress."

A sly smile spread across the sorcerer's face, but his eye remained mirthless.

"You are indeed your father's daughter, dear princess," he said, speaking the last word with heavy emphasis on the second syllable. For a moment, I felt like he doubted her title. "I did not expect so shrewd a plan from so fair a face."

He then began to set candles on the floor until they formed a large circle. Alice retreated into the shadows, away from the flame and light, while Erldan chanted. After several minutes of nasal mumbo-jumbo, the sorcerer lifted a large hourglass over his head.

"Worlds as numerous as grains of sand, send forth a champion for Princess Alice!"

Erldan flung the hourglass into the center of the circle. It shattered, and a tiny sandstorm rose from the wreckage. Suddenly, I began to cough from all the sand in my nostrils. The stuff got into my eyes as well, and sharp pains under my back made me sit up in a hurry.

And I saw her. Princess Alice. She stood before me, dressed in crimson with her brown hair braided and curled on the sides of her head, not a dream but a real person.

"Well, stand up and brush that sand off," she said. "We must hurry."

As I stood up, Erldan cleared his throat very loudly. I turned and saw that he had taken off the eyepatch, revealing not a ghastly empty socket, but a very ordinary brown eye. He now peeled off his bald pate, revealing cropped black hair underneath.

"You are truly the prince of players, Arnie," Alice said, giving him a wide smile as well as a bag that clinked. "Your performance was worth the price."

"Fortune prosper you, princess," he said, pronouncing the word in an utterly ordinary way this time, I noticed.

Alice watched him go, and when he door closed she turned to me.

"What a ham," she said. "Still, he was the best I could do under the circumstances. The better actors all belong to my father's company."

I picked up one of Erldan's books and tried to open it. It wouldn't open.

"A prop," I said.

Alice took me by the hand and started leading me to the door.

A question formed in my mind.

"If he was just an actor," I asked, "how did I get here?"

"I'm a sorceress," Alice said, as if talking to a rather dense Kindergartener. "And we have to hurry to be at the dragon's cave by second moonrise."

We left the tower by the same door the actor had, and then Alice led me to the left, and we started running through the forest.

"Shouldn't I introduce myself?" I asked.

"Your name is Ed Dolezal, and you work as a librarian," Alice said without breaking stride. "You have a tremendous fondness for dragons, although you have never seen one."

"How do you know so much?"

"I'm a sorceress, as I've already said. You don't have sorceresses in your world, but you somehow seem to know all about them."

She glanced at the night sky and then ran faster.

"I was looking for the right person to help me. After I decided you were the right one, I started sending you the dreams."

We reached a gurgling stream. A fallen tree was the only way across.

"Watch your step," she said and started walking across.

I got halfway across the tree when I thought of something.

"So if Erldan… Arnie was an actor, everything else is fake too, right? You don't have to marry Sir Blorodir? I mean, he's just another actor too?"

"He's all too real. That confrontation you saw actually did happen, but one week ago. I've been confined to the tower ever since."

She hurried off into the woods, and I followed.

Didn't she ever tire?

"Then why the charade with Erldan. I mean Arnie?"

She stopped and looked at me, an exasperated expression on her face.

"You had to want to come. I couldn't just pull you out of your world like a carrot from the dirt. You had to want to give it up."

"Give it up?"

I blinked.

"You mean I'm never going back?"

Alice approached me, her crimson dress practically glowing in the moonlight.

"Do you really want to go back to your books when you could stay here and be my champion?"

I looked at her pale skin, red hair and crimson dress. It was a compelling argument. I leaned forward to kiss her.

She turned her back on me and began hurrying through the woods again.

"We're almost there!"

I raced after her.

"Isn't this dragon's cave… dangerous?" I asked.

"No. You saw the dragon in your second dream."

"Oh."

We came to the top of a hill and looked down. A huge rocky opening lay before us. Bones lay scattered about, and chains hung from a pillar about two score paces in front of the cave's mouth.

"Come on," Alice said, taking me by the hand and leading me down. "There's nothing to be afraid of."

"You're sure?"

She smiled over her shoulder at me.

"I was born here," she said. "And this was my favorite place to play, at least until father got stuffy about it a few years ago."

I followed her and found myself at the mouth of the cave, trying to catch my breath, while she rummaged around in these trunks she had apparently kept here. I sat down with my back against a rock, while Alice chatted about how the previous occupant of the cave had carried away her pregnant mother while Daddy was away questing and Daddy had rescued them when he got back.

"Of course, spending the first months of your life in a dragon's cave does make people treat you oddly," she said as she walked over to me.

I turned and my jaw dropped.

Alice was smoking a cigar. She took a puff and sighed.

"Don't tell me you're stuffy too!" She waved the smoke away. "It's just a habit Mommy picked up during her captivity. She taught me to do it, but Daddy won't allow it in the castle any more now that Mommy's dead."

A bird shrieked three times in the forest, and Alice's eyes widened with excitement.

"It's nearly second moonrise. We better hurry."

I forced myself to my feet.

"More running?"

"No. Get out of your clothes," she said, as she began tearing her crimson gown apart.

"What are you doing?" I asked.

She handed me the cigar.

"Smoke this and get your clothes off!"

I looked at the cigar between my fingers and blinked. With a sigh, Alice took it from me, and then stuck it in my mouth. I started to cough.

"Hurry!" She said. "Get naked!"

I kicked off my shoes and slid my pants off. A glance at Alice told me that she was in the altogether. I removed my shorts.

"Into the moonlight," she said.

A second, reddish moon now appeared on the horizon. Its light made Alice look different. A strange enthusiasm filled her face as she looked at me, and I felt desire surge up in me. I tried to embrace her, but she eluded my hands and frowned. I sucked down some smoke and coughed, so I threw the cigar aside.

"You are hopeless," she said, and retrieved the cigar, puffing on it.

I grabbed her. She turned her face to me, and I kissed her, only to have her blow smoke into my mouth.

I collapsed. My arms and legs yanked this way and that in the reddish moonlight before the dragon's cave. My head began twisting from side to side as well, moved by a force that wasn't mine. Everything began to hurt.

"What are you doing to me?" I asked as I raised my head to look at Alice.

She drew on the cigar, clapped and jumped up and down. Smoke began puffing from my nostrils, and I gave my head a shake. Suddenly, something moved in my neck, and I found myself looking into Alice's blue eyes.

A moment later, I realized that my aching body still lay several feet away on the ground.

I turned my head and screamed at the sight of my enormous neck. The body it was connected to had doubled in size and continued to grow, even as its skin became a bright green.

A tail, my tail, now waved at me.

Smoke billowed from my open mouth. When it cleared, I could see that my four legs now sported viciously carved talons and yellow scales sparkled across my belly.

This was horrible, I thought. Why, I was no longer human. I was…

I was…

A dragon.

Could I breathe fire?

I tilted my head up to the night sky and released a streak of flame between the two low-hanging moons.

Roaring with delight, I became aware of Alice clinging to my neck.

"I knew you were the one." She kissed my scales. "I knew you would be my champion against Sir Blorodir. Ever since I heard Mommy's stories, I've always loved dragons."

Hoof beats clattered in the forest.

Alice laughed.

"Sir Blorodir is on time," she said, releasing me and running to the pillar.

She raised the rusty shackles and clicked them around her wrists. Then she began to shriek in a way that rattled my eardrums.

"Save me, Sir Blorodir! Save me!"

I blinked at her.

She winked.

"Don't worry," she said softly. "I want you to kill him."

"Save me! Over here!"

Moonlight glinted on armor as the knight galloped into view. As if encountering a fire breathing dragon were an everyday occurrence, Sir Blorodir set his lance at the ready and charged me.

"Save me from this crazy woman!" I wanted to yell, but it came out as a belch of fire, which the knight skillfully rode beneath as I evaded his lance.

As he galloped past, my tail instinctively took a swing at him. It only managed to clip the plume from his helmet, but the sight of that gave me confidence. If I had struck a little lower, I would have decapitated the little popinjay. Enjoying the dragoness of my changed body, I sprang to my feet and roared again.

"Bravo!" Alice clanked her chains.

Blorodir charged again, but this time I aimed my fire lower. His steed roared with pain, and I suddenly stopped, horrified by my new bloodlust.

"Kill him! Kill him!"

Now afoot, Blorodir rushed me with his sword. I reared up to blast him with fire, when I realized I might roast my hindquarters as well. I batted a scaled paw at him, and he whacked me between the talons with his blade. It hurt like a papercut magnified to the Nth.

His sword bounced off a talon and skittered out of Blorodir's hands.

"Finish him off!" Alice yanked at her chains.

The knight just stood and looked at her. I guess he had assumed that she had been yelling encouragements to him throughout the fight. I could only feel sorry for him.

If it hadn't been for the cut between my talons, I would have let him go. Instead, I leaned down and bit his head off.

Alice beamed as she cast off her shackles. "My darling dragon! My hero!"

She ran over to me, her arms outstretched, and I lowered my head to her. She kissed me on the mouth, then stepped back.

Sir Blorodir's blood was on her lips, but she smiled at me. I realized that Alice was the sickest, most evil person I had ever met. I couldn't believe I had ever found her attractive. I had let her lure me to her world and turn me into a dragon, and I didn't know what I would do now.

Alice moaned, and I looked to see her nostrils widen and her lower jaw jut forward, while her skin became a rich shade of green. Spiked scales began thrusting out from her neck, which began elongating in a most supple and delightful way. Soon, her yellow, reptilian eyes looked directly into mine. Something on the underside of my new body began stirring, and I felt embarrassed.

Alice rolled over and showed me her ruby-colored belly, and I realized that I had nothing to be ashamed of.

I had found my true love.

Summer's End

I always get blue around the end of August. It has nothing to do with the start of school, or those depressing commercials that urge you to go to Beech Point amusement park one last time before the leaves fall.

I get blue because I'm the only one who remembers the Age of Heroes. I saw it end and was right there when Fantastik fought Malvolio at Cayuga Lake Park.

I really was there, and I saw everything. I really did. It was a historic event, like Pearl Harbor or an Apollo flight.

If you had asked me before, I would have said that thousands of people would claim to have been at Cayuga Lake that day, like people always say they were part of something famous even when they weren't.

Instead, nobody cares about it. The TV, which always talks about the tenth anniversary of this, or the fifth anniversary of that, never runs any specials on it. Not like they do for the assassinations. Really, people want to act like the Age of Heroes never existed. When I try to talk about Fantastik, they give me blank looks, if not hostile stares.

Even Mom doesn't remember that day, or she won't talk about it. She was there. She took me to Cayuga Lake. Of course, her memory isn't what it used to be, but it gets me that she doesn't remember what happened that day.

Every summer, Mom would take me to Cayuga Lake Park, a nice little amusement park with a first-rate roller coaster, the Chiller. Usually, we went early in the summer, before going to Beech Point, but that summer had been really hot and uncomfortable, so we didn't go, and we didn't go. Also, my mom heard a lot of talk about how Cayuga Lake wasn't safe, with the racial situation being what it was, so I don't think she wanted to go at all.

But suddenly it was the last week of August, and we hadn't gone. Summer was almost gone, and I insisted that we go, and she gave in.

That was how I got to see the end of the Age of Heroes. I never expected to see it, in person I mean, I knew the Age of Heroes was ending. That was real clear.

It started, the end of the era, when the Golden Team seized Vorticon's Doom Machine and crashed into a comet.

Dead. Gone. More than gone. Your best friend can move to another state, and he'll never write to you again, but you know he's alive and is growing up just the same as you, and you can always hope that when you're old enough you can travel and run into him again and see how he's doing.

You can always hope.

But the Golden Team was dead. Golden Arm, Firegold, and Auricus Blaze were no more, dying in fiery agony far from the earth that they had saved.

The crazy thing was that nobody acted like anything important had happened. I'd try to talk about the death of Golden Team, and people would look at me like they wanted me to shut up. Finally I realized that nobody wanted to talk about it because it hurt too much. It was like how mom would always start to cry when I asked her about the divorce.

Even the comic book people tried to act like nothing had happened. They kept bringing out new Golden Team comics, and in one, they had the Golden Team come back from the Wraith Dimension. I wasn't fooled. They were just publishing these books because people needed to believe the Golden Team was still alive. I never bought any more Golden Team books though. I was a big boy. I could handle the truth.

Then, around Christmas, the Steel Crusader landed on Count Zorn's secret island. Zorn's son, the Shadow Hawk, rushed into battle with the Steel Crusader and got killed. Seeing that his son and hope for the future had perished, the grief-stricken Count Zorn detonated the hydrogen bomb beneath his island.

I know it was wrong of me, because Count Zorn was a supervillain, but I always admired the guy. I knew what tragedy was when I got to high school because Count Zorn was a tragic hero. He had lost his parents to the Nazis and his homeland to the Reds, and who wouldn't hate humanity after that? He kept trying to conquer the earth, and while he always failed, it was more because of unreliable underlings than the heroes against him. Year after year, Count Zorn tried to conquer the world, and you just have to admire a bastard like that.

And then the way he died, killing himself because his son was no more... who else would do something like that? Who else would value his son so much?

Not my dad.

My heroes were dying. That spring, Captain Night's heart gave out after a fight against the impetuous Lex Furon. Penitent, the young superhero pledged to live up to Captain Night's reputation and accomplishments, but I had my doubts about that.

What bothered me was that the comic book guys expected me to like Lex Furon because I'm young and he's young. I always thought Lex was a jerk. I mean, if somebody gave me superpowers, I wouldn't moan about the responsibility of it or go crazy and pick fights with other superheroes to show how tough I was. Lex Furon, superhero? More like superjerk.

Now, Captain Night, he was a real superhero. I liked him even if he went back to the Second World War, my dad's war. Maybe that's why I liked him. I could look up to Captain Night even when I couldn't look up to my dad.

Anyway, when that August rolled around, the only hero I still followed was Fantastik. I liked him because he didn't really have superpowers. He just made himself into an acrobat and warrior. When he fought somebody or climbed a building, it meant more than if Lex Furon, with his diamond-hard body, did it. Fantastik could feel pain. He was human.

That's why Malvolio was his best foe. He was human too. If Fantastik had made himself a superhero, Malvolio too had trained himself to climb, leap, fall, and use weapons, only he had done it to become a supervillain. Tried of being ignored in favor of troublemakers, Malvolio made himself into the biggest troublemaker of all.

Malvolio would form a gang, like picking a guy whose touch was electric and someone with a fake arm that could be used as a drill, then stage a big robbery. Fantastik would come after them, and Malvolio's gang would come apart, usually when it was time to split up the loot. Somehow, Malvolio would get away, but he'd always see his plans come apart, and he'd never gain a nickel from his caper.

The Fantastik vs. Malvolio feud was easily the best rivalry in comics, and that summer I could tell a new match-up between the long-time foes was in the works. Bits of Malvolio's costume, like a boot, or a glove, or the gleam from his mirrored helmet, would appear in the corner of a fame in <u>Fantastik,</u> unnoticed by everyone but me. I knew Malvolio was coming back. Finally, the cover of the latest <u>Fantastik</u> showed Malvolio and Fantastik battling each other on a roller coaster track, as a car began to roll down the hill at them.

I've never read that issue. Mom was taking me to Cayuga Lake that day, and we stopped at this store for suntan lotion. I saw Fantastik on the spinning rack, and I bought it, planning to enjoy it later.

I guess it's still in that narrow brown bag.

We left the store and drove to Cayuga Lake. The traffic was light, and we found a good parking place. We walked through the gates and ignored all the game booths on our way to the beach. After all, Mom had come here since the time there was only swimming, before they build all the rides.

Me, I didn't want to swim. I wanted to ride: the Chiller, the Scrambler, the Trabant, the Dodgems. Cayuga Lake had short lines on weekdays, so you could ride probably three times as many rides as you could at Beech Point.

So mom and I agreed that we'd meet in two hours and then see one of the shows.

Even since then, she says it was her fault. That's silly. What could she have done to stop Malvolio and Fantastik? I tell her she couldn't do anything to stop the superheroes, but she doesn't believe me.

As I walked around the park, I couldn't get the cover of the new Fantastik out of my mind. What were Fantastik and Malvolio doing at an amusement park? Then I started noticing all the money around Cayuga Lake. All the lemonade wagons, the hot dog stands, the game booths, all of those had money. Maybe that was Malvolio's plan, to rob an amusement park and take all that money.

I just got off the Dodgems and walked into the spider web shadow of the Chiller, when I heard a rattle come rushing down at my head. I looked up as the roller coaster car came clattering past, and it looked just like the hill on the cover of <u>Fantastik</u>.

Great! Fantastik and Malvolio would fight at Cayuga Lake!

I knew I had to ride the Chiller next.

This wasn't a big deal. I had ridden it by myself before, even if they always made me wait there until another single rider came along and then they paired us off together. So I wasn't scared at all.

Malvolio would try to rob Cayuga Lake, I told myself, and Fantastik would stop him.

I was going to see the end of their feud.

Even on a good day, the line for the Chiller snakes back and forth across black asphalt that just radiates heat. In mid-August, the heat is the worst, and you think your sneakers are leaving dents in the asphalt.

Tempers got short, and behind me, two guys started to argue, because one had left the line and come back to the same place. Their voices got louder, and more people began taking sides, in favor of the guy who came back and in favor of the guy who told him to go to the back of the line. I remembered my mom had heard that there had been a couple fights at Cayuga Lake this year, and I thought heading over to the Dodgems again was a good idea, when –

"Single rider! Need a single rider up here!"

Not believing my luck, I raised my hand and ran up past the line to get into the car next to an older kid. He looked at me, sighed, and then turned away from me without saying a word.

The Chiller train jolted forward.

I know I should have a better memory of what happened after that than I do. I mean, it's the most important thing in my life, right? But as often as I've tried to write it down, I can't do it in a way that feels right to me.

The train of cars jolted forward and started to curl left to climb the big hill of the coaster. over the mechanical clanking, I could hear people yelling and shouting from the line. I turned and could see a couple of guys hitting each other just before my car started getting pulled up the big hill.

I remembered Malvolio. The fight was just like something he'd plan. All the cops in the park would come to the Chiller, while he and his gang would be robbing the collection points for the park's money.

I gripped the bar in front of me, excited because I would see Malvolio's latest caper.

The front of the train reached the top of the Chiller's big hill, This was where we would start to zoom down the clattery wooden hill.

Not today. This time, we stopped.

The Chiller had <u>never</u> stopped before. All of us, in all the cars, just sat there, not knowing what to think, while the noise from below us got louder.

"A fire!"

Every head craned to look at the smoke that billowed from the base of the Chiller.

To this day, nobody knows how the fire started. I tell people Malvolio's henchmen must have lit it, as part of the diversion, and they don't pay attention to me.

I sat in my seat and could imagine fire licking the Chiller's wooden frame.

I could picture Malvolio down below, snarling in rage because his plans had gone wrong. He had used lousy accomplices again, and they had set the fire as a diversion. Needlessly hurting people was not Malvolio's way.

Fantastik would now attack him. Having pieced together the clues that led to Cayuga Lake, the hero had caught the villain. All that remained now was for them to fight.

Distracted by the fire, Malvolio had no real chance of winning. His mirrored mask shattered under the impact of Fantastik's fists just as our train began to move.

The villain fell from the track into the flames around the roller coaster track, as our train started to rattle down the hill. Fantastik stood there, looking up at us, but not seeing anything. Maybe the reflected sunlight from Malvolio's helmet had blinded him for the moment.

I screamed.

This is how it ends, I thought. Me, Malvolio, Fantastik, the whole damn age of heroes, it all ends right now.

I was lucky. The train hit the ground. The older kid next to me died, as did a few others. I'm still here to tell the story.

When I was able to talk, I asked the doctors about Fantastik. Had he made it? Only my mom knew what the hell I was talking about. The doctors and nurses got impatient with me when I kept insisting that Fantastik and Malvolio had been there that day, so I finally got the message and shut up.

I still think about him a lot, though, Fantastik. He was a good guy, a real hero, but he couldn't save us on the Chiller.

Life is like that. Stuff happens that you can't do anything about, like my mom's divorce or not being able to walk after that day at Cayuga Lake. But you go on living anyway.

The Age of Heroes is over. I was there when it ended.

Nobody admits it, however. Even mom cries when I try to talk about it. That's why I had to write this down.

I remember, and I'll always remember. I'll never forget that blind look Fantastik gave me before summer ended.

The Vegas Swingers

Chancy the Rooster lived on a farm and crowed the sunrise in every morning that he could remember. He was lord of the henhouse and ate very well, but he wasn't happy. He could watch TV, and he knew he lived in the sticks.

The real action was in Vegas.

Vegas.

Chancy could see the beckoning neon lights whenever he closed his eyes. He knew if he got there, he'd strut down the Strip with a showgirl on each arm, make a fortune singing in the showroom, making those fat suburban matrons squeal, and always win at blackjack. He'd pal around with Frankie, Dino, Sammy and the gang, maybe make a gag appearance or two in their movies, and cut a few records. He'd live, really live.

Instead, he was rotting here, in the middle of nowhere, for Farmer Jones. It killed Chancy to know that he really belonged to a Farmer Jones, a guy with the same name as all those farmers in all those brainless children's books. Good old Farmer Jones, a bigger dumb cluck than all the hens Chancy lorded it over in the henhouse. Chancy didn't know which he hated more: Farmer Jones' straw hat or his endless comments on the weather.

Still, Chancy had to admit that Farmer Jones performed one vital service. He kept Chancy out of the broiler, which was where Mrs. Jones wanted him. Fatter than any cow on the farm, Mrs. Jones thought Chancy was too old and too lazy to be rooster any more. She wanted to eat him for Sunday dinner, and she would start making noises about it every Thursday. Farmer Jones would always chuckle warmly and say he'd think about it, and then nothing would ever happen.

Then, one week, Mrs. Jones started talking on Wednesday about how good it would be to eat Chancy that Sunday. Farmer Jones did his usual chuckling, and nothing happened.

But the next week, Mrs. Jones made her speech on Tuesday. And Wednesday. And Thursday. She was in the middle of it on Friday when Farmer Jones snapped:

"If it will shut you up, Myrt, we'll eat that bird on Sunday."

Pecking outside the kitchen window, Chancy heard his fate pronounced. The unfairness of it all outraged him. To be denied a chance to seek his fortune in Vegas because of Mrs. Jones' greedy stomach! He would fight back.

He spent the night planning. He knew he couldn't fly to Vegas, and it sounded like Vegas was too far to walk to. That meant he had to steal a car.

The next day, Mrs. Jones started the car to drive to town and get the extras that would accompany Chancy on his ride into her gullet. Before she could pull out of the yard, however, Chancy headed a dozen hens in front of her car.

Mrs. Jones stuck her head out the window.

"Move! Out of my way!"

Her face turned beet red, but none of the hens moved out of her way. From the field, Farmer Jones looked at the ruckus by his house, chuckled and waved to his wife before going on about his business.

The hens ignored Mrs. Jones and stood clucking around the front of the car. Chancy had told them what to do, promising to take them to Vegas and introducing them to Frankie, Dino, and Sammy as a reward. So the more Mrs. Jones yelled and sounded the horn, the more the hens ignored her.

"You birdbrains!"

Mrs. Jones opened the car door and stepped out to shoo them away.

Just then, Chancy, clutching a trowel that Mrs. Jones had lost a few weeks ago in her flower garden, flapped down from a tree branch and whacked the farmer's wife on the head.

Mrs. Jones went down like an oak while the hens rushed about, congratulating themselves and running to the hen house for their things.

Meanwhile, Chancy flapped behind the wheel, pulled the door shut, and started for Vegas. He had no intention of keeping his promises to the hens, who, truth be told, would only be an impediment to him in Vegas.

A tank of gas may take one many places, but it could not take Chancy to Vegas. He ran out of gas after sunset and coasted the car onto the berm. He considered abandoning the vehicle and walking, but fear of coyotes and foxes made him stay with the car. He settled in under the front seat and dozed.

Chancy woke up to find the car moving again. For a panic-stricken moment, he thought he was being taken back to the Jones' farm. He soon realized this wasn't the case, but rather the car was being hauled by a very, very slow wrecker. Bit by bit, Chancy realized, he was approaching Vegas. He relaxed and decided to stay out of sight until the wrecker stopped.

Only after the car was lowered to the ground and human voices drifted away did Chancy try to get out of the Jones' car. No sooner had his claws touched the ground than he heard.

"Grrr. Who are you?"

Chancy's wings reached for the sky.

"Chancy Rooster. Who are you?"

"Grrr. Bruno the watchdog."

By now, Chancy had formed the opinion that his captor wasn't too intelligent. He glanced around and saw that he stood in an auto junkyard.

"My good dog, I didn't mean to steal anything. I simply want to go to Vegas. If you want to come with me, I'd be more than happy. I can introduce you to Frankie and Dino."

"You know Frankie and Dino?" An impressed note was in the dog's voice.

"Best of friends," Chancy said, knowing it was a lie.

He turned and came face to face with a huge brown dog whose tongue seemed bigger than his head as it hung past yellowing teeth.

"Come with me," Chancy said, "and I'll show you more fun in a week than you've had in ten years guarding this junk."

Bruno's eyes narrowed as he looked the rooster over.

"What about chicks?" he asked. "Can you fix me up with some of them gorgeous Vegas chicks?"

"You'll be walking down the Strip with one on each arm."

Bruno's eyes went out of focus as he considered the prospect. Finally, he swallowed.

"I'm going to Vegas with you," he said. "Follow me."

He trotted over to a pickup truck sitting by the junkyard gate with its windows rolled down. Chancy followed and noticed a rifle hanging in the truck's rear window. Bruno nodded at the pickup.

"Get in the truck and wait for me."

Chancy flapped his wings and scuttled in, then paced nervously along the torn upholstery. He hated trusting his future in Vegas to this dopey dog, but he couldn't see any other way at present. Besides, the keys weren't in the truck.

A huge noise erupted from the junkyard's office, starting with a scream that was swiftly followed by a shower and curses and a few gunshots. Chancy saw Bruno leaped from the office window with a set of keys in his mouth. The bald junkyard owner hobbled out the front door, trying, and failing, not to put too much weight on his right leg. When he did so, another shower of curses erupted from his lips.

"Bruno, you ungrateful mutt! I'm going to kill you!"

By now, Bruno had started the truck, and the two fugitives were on their way to the bright lights of Vegas. The bald man fired a badly aimed shot, fell over, and cursed again.

Bruno laughed, letting his tongue flap out the side window.

"Always knew he couldn't shoot."

Chancy leaned over and looked at the gas gauge. His spirits fell again.

"Half a tank? Vegas is farther away than that!"

Bruno smiled, showing his yellowed teeth.

"We'll get more," he said. "I've got it all worked out."

Whenever Bruno spotted a likely gas station, preferably a busy one, he'd slow down and let Chancy hop out. Then he'd drive around the block a few times, letting Chancy sprint ahead to the station. The rooster would start to strut and crow, and before long people would be staring at this crazy bird acting like nothing they had ever seen before, while Bruno would fill up the truck and pull away. He'd wait for Chancy a couple of blocks down the road, and they'd be off.

The first three times, the scam worked like a charm. The fourth time they needed gas, they were in the desert, and the only gas station in sight had no business at all. Dirt caked its big neon sign, and Bruno nearly drove past, not quite sure if the place were open.

"Do your thing, rooster," Bruno said. "This is our only chance."

"Isn't there anyplace else?"

"Not around here." Bruno shook his head. "The only thing we've got in the tank is vapors, and I'd hate to run out of gas out there."

He motioned at the heat rising from the desert highway.

Chancy shrugged and leaped out of the truck. Bruno slowed down and let the rooster run to the station and go into his act. Chancy leaped and strutted and sang "I'm Just Wild About Harry," one of the songs he hoped to do in Vegas.

Nobody clapped. Nobody came out to look at this crazy rooster.

The lack of response troubled Chancy. He stopped his antics and listened. He could hear a voice from inside, saying that the story you were about to see was true.

Bruno pulled up and started pumping gas. He had just started to relax when he heard the sound of a revolver being cocked behind him.

"Just how are you going to pay for this gas, mutt?"

Bruno gave a longing look at the rifle in the back of the pickup and then raised his arms and turned to face an orange tom cat who held a gun on him. Bruno's legs began to shake.

"That tuneless rooster in with you too?" the cat asked.

"Yes, I am," Chancy said as he hurried over. "We didn't want to hurt anyone. We're just on our way to Vegas." He flashed a smile at the cat. "We could take you with us, you know."

"That's right." Bruno's tongue flapped. "Chancy knows Frankie and Dino."

Chancy winced. That did not seem like the right line to use on this cat.

Bruno didn't notice but just chattered on. "And when we get to Vegas, we'll all have a great time and meet a lot of chicks."

The cat looked unimpressed.

"If you two know Frankie and Dino, I'm a bosom pal of Mickey Mouse."

"Hey, no kidding?" Bruno asked.

"So what?" Chancy sneered at the cat. "Do you think what you have here is better than what we can get in Vegas?"

The cat didn't answer. The sound of the I Love Lucy theme floated out from the gas station window.

"That slob." The cat hissed. "I do all the work around here, while he watches reruns. It'd serve him right if I ran off."

Chancy and Bruno sighed with relief.

"Finish gassing that thing up," the cat said. "I'm going to clean out the cash register. Bankrolling me in Vegas is the least that slob can do for me after all these years."

When the cat returned, he found Chancy in the truck, while Bruno, nervous, stood next to the door.

"Do you mean he doesn't really know Frankie or Dino?" Bruno asked, after a nervous glance at Chancy.

The cat looked confused for a moment, then he smiled.

"Of course he knows Frankie and Dino. I'm Felix the Cat after all. I used to be a friend of Mickey's back in the old neighborhood before he got a big head and forgot about his old pals, the jerk."

Cat and dog got in the truck and set out for Vegas.

The next day, as they drove up a hill, the truck sputtered and began to lose speed. Bruno pressed the gas pedal again and again, but the truck ran slower and slower, finally stopping.

"We've got plenty of gas," Bruno complained.

Felix hissed.

"You stupid mutt. I bet you never looked under the hood of this thing. Now you've got us stuck in the desert."

"We can't be too far from Vegas," Chancy said. "We can hitchhike or walk or something."

Bruno, eager to get off the hook, nodded. "That's right. We can still get to Vegas even if the truck can't."

An hour later, none of them took their arrival in Vegas for granted. The sun beat down without mercy, the ground burned their feet, and the few motorists who came down the road refused to stop for a rooster, a dog and a cat.

Nauseated from the heat, Chancy shut his eyes and swayed. How nice if he could fall over, he thought. He had escaped Mrs. Jones' frying pan only to ended up baked in the desert.

He had to go on.

Chancy opened his eyes and saw a horse on the top of the hill in front of them, just like in a Western. He blinked, thinking it was a dream, but the horse still stood there.

"Hey! Hey!"

Felix and Bruno joined in the yelling, and finally the horse sauntered over.
"What's the hubbub?"

"Our truck broke down," Chancy said, not trusting his companions with the talking, "and we're trying to get to Vegas."

"Vegas? What's that?"

"Las Vegas." Felix smiled with all his fake charm.

No recognition chimed in the horse's eyes.

"Never heard of it. But is it in that direction?" A flip of his tail indicated the West.

"Yes!" Chancy, Bruno and Felix all shouted.

"Good. I'll take you there. I'd even take you east or south as well. I just won't go north. My master's up there, and he wants to sell me to a glue factory."

"There are no glue factories in Vegas," Felix said.

"Sounds like a friendly town," the horse said. "Climb on board and point me in the right direction."

So the four would-be swingers headed to Vegas.

In Vegas, the most important man in the city, Cadillac Tony, was having problems. Some of these were not his fault, such as the fact that the Neon Cowgirl's horse was so lame she couldn't ride the strip for a month. Some of these problems were his fault, such as the fact that he had been skimming the take from the casinos and Lucky had begun to get suspicious.

Concrete (the very word made Cadillac Tony wince) proof of Lucky's suspicion was Pittsburgh Pete, who walked around the slots and tables counting the suckers and wondering why the numbers were off. Watching Pete on closed-circuit TV, Cadillac Tony wondered what Pete's price was and how high it would be.

Then something he saw on the screen made Cadillac Tony leap from his chair.

A cat was playing one of the slots.

That had never even happened in the back of the Brooklyn candy store where Cadillac Tony had gotten his start. His finger hit the button on the intercom.

"Get that cat out of my casino!"

"But he's with me."

Turning, Cadillac Tony confronted a preening rooster.

"Chancy Rooster," the bird said, before starting to croon "Everybody Loves Somebody Sometime."

Chancy had just gotten the word "somehow" out when Cadillac Tony's hands closed over his windpipe.

"Chicken, the only way you're coming back in my casino is as a main course. You and your lousy friends aren't welcome here."

Al the Goon appeared in the doorway, with Felix in one hand and Bruno in the other. The sleeves of his jacket were in tatters.

"I caught this dog placing a bet at the roulette table," he said. "Uh, what's going on?"

"How do I know? Just dump 'em outside and let me have some peace and quiet. That rooster's the leader, so give him something to think about. I need time to think about what to do with the guy about the S-K-I-M."

Al called for Artie, and the two goons carried the friends out through the casino's kitchen, being sure, as Cadillac Tony had instructed, to give Chancy a long look at the row of plucked and decapitated poultry before dumping them outside in the trash.

"Gee," Felix said from under some spoiled parsley, "I'm surprised you didn't tell them about how you're pals with Frankie, Sammy, and Dino, Mr. Big Hot Shot Rooster."

Just then they heard a clip-clop, clip-clop. It was the horse. While Chancy, Felix and Bruno were covered in garbage, the horse sported a new saddle decorated with bright neon tubes.

"This is a sure friendly town," the horse said. "I was just walking down the street looking at all the lights, and a woman yelled

'That's my new Buckaroo!' Then she took me and fed me and gave me this saddle."

Chancy leaned his head back against the wall.

"I don't believe this."

"She's nice, but she insists on calling me Buckaroo," the horse said. He shook his head. "Apart from that, it isn't too bad. It looks like it will be a long-term job too, since she isn't going with Mr. Tony."

"Cadillac Tony? He's going someplace?" Felix asked.

"Rio de Janero. He asked my boss if she wanted to go with him, but she laughed and said there was no place to get away from Lucky."

"The skim," Chancy said softly.

"Well, the sun's going down, and I've got to get to work," the horse said. He flicked his tail. "You fellas got jobs yet?"

"We have one job lined up," Felix said. "Just one job, and then we retire."

"Good luck, then."

The horse clip-clopped away.

A few hours later, Cadillac Tony sat in his office, drumming his fingers on the suitcase that contained the skimmed cash, waiting for Al and Artie the Goons to take him to the airport while a grease fire in the kitchen distracted Pittsburgh Pete.

Cadillac Tony patted the shoulder holster under his jacket. At the airport, he would pay off Al and Tony and then fly to Rio.

He chuckled. The Neon Cowgirl didn't know what she was missing.

The fire alarm started to wail. Cadillac Tony smiled. This was the signal. Everything had started smoothly. He stood up and walked over to the door.

No sooner had he turned the knob, than the door swung in at him, and three screaming animals leaped at him.

Cadillac Tony pulled his pistol and tried to strike the rooster scratching at his head, but he dropped the suitcase of money. The dog grabbed the handle in his teeth and fled, and the cat bit Tony's hand, making him drop the gun.

The animals fled as Tony scooped up the gun and started shooting. His shots slammed into the doorjamb just as Al and Artie arrived. Instinct took over, and the two goons returned fire, drilling Cadillac Tony. As he breathed his last, Al and Artie took in the situation. They were in big trouble, and only the missing suitcase could get them out, whether into Pittsburgh Pete's good graces or the good life in Rio didn't matter. They needed the suitcase.

By now the three bandits had reached the main floor of the Casino and had gotten onto the Strip. Tourists pointed at them and laughed, thinking it was all some crazy stunt.

"If only we had that stupid horse to carry us," Bruno wheezed. "This is heavy."

"Don't let go of that!"

Chancy pointed ahead of them, where two white-haired women were getting out of a Lincoln at a valet parking stand.

"There!"

Felix flung himself at the valet, who fell to the ground. Bruno bounded into the car, with Chancy right behind. The rooster grabbed the suitcase.

"Get in the back seat," he said, clutching the case as if it contained all his dreams.

Felix scrambled into the car, pulled the door shut, and drove away from the Neon Wasteland into the desert, chuckling like a maniac.

A couple hours later, when they were under the desert stars, Felix glanced up into the mirror and saw a pair of headlights behind him.

"Somebody's tailing us."

"Go faster, willya!" Chancy said.

Felix pressed down on the pedal, but the car continued to cruise along.

"This bucket of bolts won't go any faster," Felix said.

Bruno snored in the backseat.

The headlights followed them all through the night, no matter how many roads Felix turned down to try and lose his pursuers. As the sun rose, their car had long since left the pavement and was bumping over gravel.

"That a sign?" Felix asked, pointing at a large dark object between himself and the rising sun. "Can't read it."

"Bridge out, you fool."

Chancy cackled as he kicked his door open and leaped out from the car, pulling the suitcase behind him.

Seconds later, Felix and Bruno plunged off a cliff, Felix cursing all the way down. Al the Goon tried to slam on his brakes the moment he saw their red taillights disappear, but he had been following too closely, and so he and Artie followed the cat and the dog to the grave.

Chancy stood on the edge of the cliff, looked down at the burning wreckage and crowed. It was too bad about Felix and Bruno, he thought, but money divided one way went farther than money divided three ways.

By noon, however, Chancy realized that he needed a partner so he could get the money to someplace where he could spend it. Pulling the suitcase through the desert by himself would be too much for him.

"I need a partner, a stupid one," he said.

Chancy could try to talk to a coyote or a snake, but they would probably cheat him. He needed a partner he could cheat.

Then he remembered Farmer Jones. Chancy couldn't think of anyone dumber than Farmer Jones. All he had to do was get back to the farm, tell Farmer Jones where he had hidden a million bucks, and then find a way to cheat the slob after the hard work of getting the money out of the desert had been done.

Crowing at his own brilliance, Chancy set about covering the suitcase with stones. Then he found two pieces of wood and formed them into a cross, putting it at the head of the pile of stones. Now it looked like a pioneer's grave in one of those TV Westerns Farmer Jones always watched. Nobody would disturb it.

The idea of how rich he would be when he got home kept Chancy moving his feet through the desert. The trip back to the farm took more effort than the trip out. There was no Bruno or Felix or horse to help out this time. Chancy walked, hopped freight trains, and walked some more. Finally, one day around sunset, the green hills he walked through became familiar.

A hen clucked in Farmer Jones' front yard as Chancy walked up.

"Hello, Penny," Chancy said.

"Chancy! Why, we'd thought we'd seen the last of you! What happened to Farmer Jones' car?"

"Gone. But he can buy a new one, ten new ones, with all the money I have for him."

Penny's eyes narrowed.

"Where's this money? In your gullet?"

"In Vegas. I've got a cool million in a suitcase in Vegas, and I'll share it with him if he takes me there."

Blinking, Penny recalled other promises Chancy had made.

"I see," she said. "You must be tired from your trip. You rest under this tree, and I'll get Farmer Jones."

"Thank you, Penny," Chancy said as he sat under the elm tree.

He marveled that he still had the hens in love with him. He shook his head. His talents were just wasted on this farm. He belonged in the big time. He should be running Vegas instead of just singing there.

Human footsteps neared, and Chancy looked up expecting to see Farmer Jones' stupid face.

The red face of Mrs. Jones glared down at the rooster, who started to scream.

"A million dollars in cash! I can take you to it!"

The farmer's wife's left hand closed around the rooster's throat and pulled him up into the air. Her strong right hand gripped his head and quickly wrung his neck.

"A rooster with a million dollars. Whoever heard of anything so stupid? You good-for-nothing rooster. You'll be better use for Sunday dinner than you ever were in your life."

And she was right.

The Garden Dwellers

I live in the garden.

But I feel that I shouldn't.

At night I dream, and in my dreams I'm not alone. In my dreams, people surround me, hurrying here and there. Sometimes they talk to me, but I cannot see their faces. Yet it seems right to me to be among people.

There is something unnatural about my situation. Man is meant to live in society.

During the day, I am alone in the garden. I explore it. I have not yet found where the garden ends. I climb tall trees, but from my perch I simply see more of the gentle green expanse of the garden. Occasionally, I see some blue, but when I get there it always turns out to be nothing but a large pond.

The ponds here are never deep. I wade through them, and the water never comes to more than halfway up my knee. The water is always warm and pleasant, even when I wake near a pond and rush into it first thing in the morning.

I know cold and chill, but I do not know how I know them from the garden, where such things do not exist.

It never rains in the garden. I know this is wrong, for the leaves and flowers are always fresh and colorful. If it truly never rained here, I know the leaves would be withered and the grass brown.

I know that, and yet, as with cold and chill, I don't know *how* I know that. All my life has been in the garden.

It is a beautiful place. Flowers and bushes are everywhere. Tulips bloom after sunrise and mums before sunset. Roses bloom when the sun stands overhead and shadows are at their smallest. The trees bear apples and oranges, so I have no hunger.

How do I know that word, hunger, if I cannot experience it here?

From my dreams, perhaps?

I do not like my dreams. They are not pleasant. Everyone moves so quickly. People walk about so fast that I cannot see their faces. No one looks at me but simply walks past me.

But they must see each other's faces, I think. Once in a while, two people will walk close to each other, hold hands, and look at each other. I cannot see their faces, but I think they must see each other's faces.

It angers me. Why don't any of my dream people stop to look at me? Often I wonder if there is something wrong with me, and they know what it is.

Other times I wonder if I am in the garden as punishment.

I usually wake from my dreams saddened. The garden is beautiful, but my dreams tell me that it is wrong. I am hiding here, when I should live in society and hurry like the people in my dreams.

I should be busy.

When the dreams first came, I would wake up and determine to be busy. I explored the garden, looking for its end. I would try to fashion tools from the tree branches.

I never found the garden's end. When I would wake up, the tools I had fashioned the day before would be gone.

The dreams still upset me, but I no longer wake up and charge off to try to be busy. Instead, I lie in a pond and let its warmth cover me. My face rises above the warmth and I try to think of person who would see my face.

When the bad feeling from the dream passes, I get out of the pond and walk about. Sometimes I go toward the sun. Sometimes I go away from it.

Today is different. Today, when my feelings from the dream are gone, and I get out of the pond, I see a footprint in the mud by the pond. It is not my footprint. It is smaller.

My heart begins beating faster. Would I be able to see someone's face today?

I run in the direction the footprint pointed. Every so often, I see a footprint or some beaten down grass, and I continue to follow.

Someone will see my face.

I run across the garden. The sun rises high in the sky, yet I still run on, past tulips, past roses, and finally past mums.

There she stands.

Behind golden mums that came up to her waist, she stands smiling at me. Her reddish hair hangs down over her tanned, strong shoulders. Her pale blue eyes meet mine with confidence.

I can see her face.

And she smiled at me.

Fear closes on my heart. What if she doesn't like me?

"Friend?" I ask.

"Friend," she says, and she steps toward me, holding out her hands.

I close my hands around hers and pull her close to me.

"Can you see my face?" I ask.

She smiles and kisses me.

"I can," she says, and we kiss again.

We embrace, and I know that my dreams will not trouble me again. She leaps up and throws her legs around me. I nearly fall, but I keep hold of her and until I kneel.

She lays back on the ground, and we make love.

I will be lonely never again.

I lay there, holding her hand, and I want to know more about her. How did she get here? Why are we so fortunate?

"What is your name?" I ask.

She laughs.

"Eve," she says. She runs a finger around my nipple. "And I shall call you Adam."

My fears return. I know of Adam and Eve, the first man and the first woman. They lived in the Garden of Eden until God drove them out.

If she were truly Eve, and I were truly Adam, I would not know *about* Adam and Eve and the rest of their story. I have only lived in the garden. I have not read any books, seen any movies.

But how do I know about books and movies?

"I guess we shouldn't eat any apples," I say.

Eve laughs and rolls on top of me to kiss me. Even as my body responds to hers and we begin to make love again, I know I remember that laugh. I have heard it before.

How could I, if I have always lived in the garden?

That night we sleep, and I dream again. She is in my dream, but we are not in the garden. We are in the society of my dreams. We walk along together, like any other couple, but the faceless people do not treat us like any other couple. They look at us, whisper, laugh, and begin to form a circle around us.

We turn and try to walk away, but the circle of faceless ones is all around now. They make noises at us, and I know that they hate us.

I wake in the garden and reach for Eve. She lies next to me, asleep, her face untroubled.

Why do I dream bad dreams, and she does not?

A day passes as we explore the garden, calling each other Adam and Eve. As lovely as the garden is, I find her more beautiful. Her coppery hair and tan face bring me joy each time I look at them. She sees me watching her instead of the trees, and I blush with embarrassment.

"There are only the two of us here," she says. "Why be embarrassed? I love you, and you love me."

She takes my hand and draws me close to her.

"I never want to be lonely again," I say.

"If we are brave," she says, "we need never be lonely again."

Before sleep that night, I think over her words again. Why "brave"? The garden is a place without danger. I have never seen a snake or any animal here. Only Eve shares the garden with me. I find no danger in her.

The only danger I feel comes from my dream of last night.

How can a dream be dangerous?

Unless it is real, the answer comes to my mind. I bat it away.

As soon as I fall asleep, Eve and I are back among the angry, faceless people. They stand closer tonight than they did last night. They yell at us, but I can't understand their words. We try to break free, but they press in on us, forcing us to stand back to back, and still they press against us, with their hatred, that we cannot breathe.

I awake, gasping for breath. Eve, her face serene, sleeps beside me.

I look and wonder why she is not afflicted like me. I resent it, that she can sleep without fear. I shake her.

"What's wrong?" she asks.

"Bad dreams," I say, and then hate myself for sounding childish.

Eve takes my hand and looks worried. I pull away from her.

"I dreamed we were in a crowd that hated us."

Eve blinks rapidly and looks away. She is worried now, and I feel ashamed.

"Dreams! I never thought…"

She doesn't finish her idea but smacks her fist against the earth. After a while, she turns back to me, a smile on her face.

"If we are brave, Adam, we need never be lonely again."

Eve takes my hand and places it on her breast. I smile at her, and we embrace.

I pass a dreamless night, but Eve is awake when I rise. For the first time since I met her, she is unhappy, although she smiles when she sees me. Worry lines cross the skin around her blue eyes.

"How did you sleep?"

"Fine," I say. "No dreams."

She kisses me.

"We must be brave," she says. Then she stands. "We should go to that big pond we saw yesterday."

She starts walking. I stand up and follow her, but as I draw near to her, she starts walking faster. I walk faster too, and as I reach for her hand, she starts to run. I run as well, and soon we are both laughing as we approach the big pond.

Eve splashes into the pond and turns to face me. I run to her and embrace her. We kiss, and then she throws her arms around my neck and falls backward into the water. I land on top of her, but still we kiss.

She pulls away from me and hurries to the shore. I follow, and she smiles at me. We make love on the edge of the pond.

After, we look up at the sky. Eve raises a hand to her mouth and complains.

"If only we had cigarettes. That's something I forgot."

Immediately I know what a cigarette is, although I know I've never seen on in the garden. I grab Eve's hand.

"What's going on? Why do I know about Adam and Eve, cigarettes, and things that I couldn't possibly, shouldn't know about? What did you mean by saying you forgot about cigarettes or hadn't thought about dreams? What is happening here?"

Eve can't speak. Instead a sadness, deep and terrible, wells up within those blue eyes as she looks at me.

"Promise you'll be brave, Paul?" she asks.

"Of course," I say, but at the sound of my name, a cold wind begins to blow through the garden, killing the blooms of the tulips, the roses and the mums. Petals shrivel and fall by the thousands as a chill rain falls from the skies, and an automobile horn blares.

I am Paul.

Rain makes my shirt wet and cling to my shoulders.

I am Paul, not Adam.

The rain beats down harder and I see it bounce off the sidewalk.

"Who are you?" I ask the woman, as the red fades from her hair, leaving dishwater blonde with a few streaks of gray.

"Cheryl," she says, as crows feet circle her eyes and wrinkles furrow across her forehead.

She fishes a cigarette and a lighter out of her purse and lights up.

It is Cheryl, not Eve, who stands before me. Plump and sagging, she puffs hurriedly and tries to smile bravely.

I know I am not the heroic Adam, but rather the stooped, spectacle-wearing Paul who stands open-mouthed before her, waiting for some explanation.

"It was magic, Paul," she says. "I knew you were nervous about the difference between our ages." She gives me a look, draws on the cigarette and blows the smoke out in exasperation.

"I just thought that if we could meet in a place were that didn't matter, and if we fell in love there, you would love me here. That's why I created the garden for us."

By now, several umbrella-wielding people have stopped to look at us. I recognize some of them, fellow graduate students of Cheryl's and mine. They are the ones who laugh first.

I glance at Cheryl, each sign of age on her face now gigantic. I remember how she told her daughter had just entered college as a freshman.

I am closer to her daughter than I am to her.

"They can't be a couple," a woman's voice says. "She could be his mom."

I shut my eyes and remember the fun I had with Cheryl before I woke in the garden, fun talking with her about the books we'd read and the books we wanted to write.

"Talk about an odd couple," a male voice says from behind me.

"She's too old for him," a woman says.

I want to say something. I want to move, but I can't beyond opening my eyes.

Cheryl searches my face for a sign. Seeing none, she drops her cigarette to the sidewalk and runs away from me. I lose sight of her as the umbrellas move around while people stare at me, until they lose interest and walk away.

Oddly, no one congratulates me on abandoning Cheryl.

I turn and head back to my apartment.

It would never have worked out with Cheryl, I tell myself each time I see a couple of people who are the same age. It would not have worked out.

I slow down and let the couples pass me. Time isn't that important now.

I watch a couple walk past me under one umbrella. They laugh at something, and I try to think of the garden.

Cheryl and me would have never worked, I try to tell myself. Ask anybody.

I live in society.

I am alone.

Snoozing Doozie

Snoozing Doozie? You want to know if this is <u>the</u> Hattonville where Snoozing Doozie lived?

It is. Of course, you aren't stupid because you had to ask. I mean, I've traveled a bit, and I know Hattonville is just like any other town in America. Mac-Mart on the outskirts of town, closed up stores downtown, Burger Shit and Taco Hell on the strip, teenagers smoking dope under the Civil War monument.

No, I'm not running for office.

I get the picture. You don't want to know how things <u>are</u>. You want to know how things <u>were</u>.

Well, you have a choice. You can drive three blocks and go to the Snoozing Doozie house, pay five bucks to look at some old furniture and hear a bunch of lies, then buy a Snoozing Doozie T-shirt and some syrupy pop in a souvenir glass for a godawful amount of money, or you can sit in the shade with me, and I'll tell you the truth about this town. And I won't sell you anything.

Good. I could tell you were more intelligent than the other tourists who come here from the way you stopped at the red light before turning right.

Now the whole Snoozing Doozie business started back when Warren G. Harding was President.

No, he wasn't the one who got stuck in the bathtub. That was Taft. You must have studied history in college to know about that. You know, I like you more and more.

You understand, Harding never laid eyes on Snoozing Doozie. I just start the story with him to let you know when it started.

Today the name Hattonville doesn't mean anything. Back then, it meant everything. The Hattons owned the bank, and nothing happened in town that they didn't want to have happen. There were two of them, Mr. James and Miss Elaine. Brother and sister. They hated each other worse than they hated Elmo Peters, the teller who ran off with $800 in Aught-Seven.

Never heard of what happened to Elmo Peters. You aren't his grandson, are you?

Anyway, they hadn't always hated each other. They had been the most loving brother and sister until Mr. James went to college and came home with a wife. That made 'em enemies.

Miss Elaine couldn't stand the sight of Mrs. Rosalind, Mr. James' wife. She wouldn't let 'em stay one night at the old Hatton place – that's the firebombed place with the graffiti you saw when you drove in on the fourlane. Of course, it was a lot better kept up when Miss Elaine was alive. Anybody Miss Elaine'd catch writing on her house wouldn't write anything else, ever.

So Mr. James and his new wife spent that night and all the other nights at the hotel until they built the new Hatton place, what you know as the Snoozing Doozie house. When we're done here, you can walk down and take a photo of the Snoozing Doozie house. It's a pretty place, and they haven't figured out a way to charge folks for just taking a picture of it. I give 'em a few more years until they do.

That marriage, like I said, started the hatred between Mr. James and Miss Elaine. She never wore anything but black from that day too. She fired all of her people who had laid eyes on Miss Rosalind or mentioned her name. She put a big iron fence around her yard, and she planted red roses with the biggest thorns anyone had ever seen around the house.

Mr. James, well, he didn't care. He acted like everything was right as rain. He still met Miss Elaine when it came time to do the bank's business, but he never mentioned her clothes or the black veil she wore. He even invited her over to his new house, when it was done. She would go, but gossip was that she would always arrive late, to Thanksgiving dinner, to Christmas, to what-have-you, and sit there like a spider on a wedding cake, not saying a word, until she left.

Life went on, although folks noticed that the town itself was moving toward Mr. James. New buildings went up near his house, and fires broke out a lot near Miss Elaine's. Her neighbors on both sides got burned out that first year of the feud, and they rebuilt near Mr. James. Miss Elaine just planted roses on those vacant lots.

Mr. James and Mrs. Rosalind had a daughter, and they named her Celestine. That's Snoozing Doozie, and I guess that's easier to say than Celestine. Easier to spell, anyway. Folks that name a child Celestine are just asking for trouble.

If Mr. James could act like there was no feud with Miss Elaine, and Mrs. Rosalind could act like there was no Miss Elaine, Celestine couldn't. She hated Miss Elaine from the cradle. Miss Elaine would step across the threshold, and that baby would let go with all the screeching she could. Miss Elaine would send toys over, and within the hour they'd be broken and tossed in the trash.

I don't know why she did it. I mean Miss Elaine sending those toys. Ever since Celestine was born, she wanted that baby to love her. I truly think she did. Maybe it was just because Celestine was a Hatton after all.

But Celestine would never love Miss Elaine.

Once, I remember, Miss Elaine sent for a doll from overseas. It was made out of that stuff they make dishes out of, starts with a P, and Celestine just took that doll outside, set it on a tree branch and let it fall down and smash to pieces.

Porcelain? Sounds a bit like Celestine, doesn't it?

I saw you look at your watch. We're almost at the Snoozing Doozie curse now. That doll gift happened when Celestine was ten or so. A couple years later, Celestine's twelfth birthday came up.

That's what I hate about what the Snoozing Doozie thing has done. Tourists from all over the country come here to find out about Snoozing Doozie, and when they get to her house, they look and see that the back yard is just a parking lot. It makes me sick.

Back then, the back yard was a yard. Big shady trees with swings hanging from sturdy branches. A metal slide that stood over six foot tall. One of them big gliding swings that four grownups could sit on at once. Every child in Hattonville wanted to play there, among those shady trees.

But we couldn't, you see, not unless Celestine asked us. And she usually didn't. Mr. James, however, he invited us all over for Celestine's birthday. We could swing and climb trees and eat ice cream. It was like Heaven.

Everybody knew Celestine's twelfth birthday would be the best of all. We just knew it and looked forward to it more than to Christmas.

Nobody knew that day would cause all the trouble.

Damn idiots had to bulldoze that yard over and make it a parking lot. If I hadn't spent all my life here, I'd move.

Yes, yes, the birthday party. Well, every year, Miss Elaine was invited to Celestine's birthday party, she being Celestine's aunt and all. That's how Celestine got the doll. Every year Miss Elaine would come, dressed in black, and sit by herself until she left at sundown. She never bothered us, but she was pretty scary, dressed for a funeral like that.

Anyway, this year Celestine put her foot down and told Mr. James that she did not want Miss Elaine at her birthday party. She said she would rather go without a birthday party at all than have that old black spider ruin it.

Now that was the first time in her life that Celestine had talked to Mr. James like that. He knew she was serious, and as soon as she finished talking, Mrs. Rosalind started in on how Miss Elaine had never once shown her courtesy. Mr. James knew that this was true, and the burden of always trying to be nice to his sister Miss Elaine, despite her cold behavior, became too much.

They sent a man to tell Miss Elaine not to come to Celestine's birthday party.

She came anyway.

The old black spider walked across town and stood on the sidewalk in front of Mr. James' house and looked at us children. We couldn't play with her watching us like that, and Celestine started to cry. Mr. James went out front and told Miss Elaine to leave.

She said nothing to him but just walked back across town, went into the old Hatton house, and never came out. A week after the party, Mr. James and Doc Barton went in there and found her body.

Nobody moved into that house. The roses she planted lost their blooms and just grew thorns. On the other hand, a year after Miss Elaine's funeral, a big red rose bush grew out of her grave. Nobody knew who planted it.

Celestine had been growing too. Without Miss Elaine around, she was a much happier girl, and by her sixteenth birthday, everybody knew a prettier girl could not be found in the County. We all envied Sam Barton, the doctor's son, who would take her to the picture show in Weston for her birthday.

You probably drove through Weston on your way here. It ain't nothing now, but then, back in those Depression days, it was the place to go if you had some spare money to spend on your girl.

Well, beautiful as she was, with the doctor's son wrapped around her finger, Celestine wanted more. She wanted a corsage of red roses.

Yes, roses from Miss Elaine's grave.

Why didn't we stop her? Hell, who knew what would happen? Did you ever hear of anything like this happening anywhere else before?

Hector and me had the job of keeping the cemetery neat. We had just finished cutting the grass, and not with a gas-powered mower either, you mind, when we saw Celestine come marching through the gates, scissors in hand. She went straight up to Miss Elaine's grave, reached over to get a rose, and a thorn pricked her. She keeled over, and I thought she was dead.

Hector ran over to look at her. He yelled for me to go get Mr. James or Doc Barton or somebody, and I sure was glad to run out of that cemetery.

Mr. James was standing in his front yard, looking like he knew something bad had happened even before I reached his house. Maybe he knew what Celestine had wanted to do, I don't know. I barely gasped out my news before he charged down the street like the Light Brigade. Then I ran for Doc Barton.

So I didn't see this next thing myself, but Hector told me that when Mr. James got to the cemetery and saw Celestine on the ground, he didn't even stop to hear Hector say that Celestine was still alive. Mr. James just tore into that rose bush with his bare hands, like he would wrestle it, cursing like a man possessed. At first, Hector thought he was pulling it out by the roots, but then he saw that the bush was growing and wrestling Mr. James right back. It wound itself around his neck, the thorns tore his skin, and he choked to death.

They weren't the only roses growing that hour. The thorns from around Miss Elaine's house must have started growing around the time Celestine pricked her finger. They grew across the road to Weston and they pulled down the phone lines. I could hear the poles breaking as I got back to the cemetery with Doc Barton and Sam.

Doc Barton looked Celestine over. He said she was alive, but he didn't know how to wake her. When Sam heard those words, he went crazy. He shouted that he'd get the medicine that would save her, and he ran to his father's Model A and took off like a bat out of hell, driving down the Weston road, right into those thorns.

Last we saw of Sam was the thorns closing over his car. Never found his body until, you know, when that singer came. Hector and me talked about Sam a lot in the next few years. We never knew that he loved Celestine that much.

How many bodies were there in the thorns when it was all over? Damn, if that isn't the question all you tourists ask.

Seven. Five of 'em were people trying to get out of Hattonville. Either they thought they could make it, like Sam, or they had had enough and just went thorn-happy like Mrs. Rosalind. Two of the, were from the outside trying to get in. Never knew who they were or why they thought getting in would be a good idea.

Hell, I wish anyone would have got through the thorns instead of that singer.

Anyway, none of us would have survived without Doc Barton. Those idiots who run the Snoozing Doozie museum have a picture of him in there, all right, but it's only as big as a postage stamp. They've got plenty of pictures of that singer, but that's because all the tourists have heard of him.

Doc Barton, he was the one who really saved Hattonville. There we were, surrounded by thorns. We couldn't get in, and we couldn't call out. The thorns had messed up the phone wire, and we could only get static on the radio. We might have panicked. We might have rushed into those thorns and killed ourselves trying to get out. We might have gotten depressed and just sat around waiting to die.

But we didn't. Doc Barton saved us. He took over and ran the town. He gave everyone a job to do: gardening, canning food, exercising. He kept us happy, and we got through the ordeal.

No, not everybody. Something lasts that long, you're going to lose people. I said five people from town ended up in the thorns, but that includes Sam, who still thought he could get out, and Mrs.

Rosalind, who went into the thorns because she didn't have anyone left. I tell you, it could have been worse. All of us could have died.

Doc Barton kept us going. Years passed, but we didn't know it. The whole town missed the Second World War, although we were living under tighter rationing than anywhere else in the country. We missed Korea too, although most folks don't find that nearly as remarkable.

I guess there were a few attempts to rescue us. I mean, we did find the bodies of those two fellas in the thorns when the whole business was over. We never heard 'em, though, and never could identify 'em either.

Celestine? Well, Doc Barton realized that she was alive, but in a coma, he said, since the day it started. We carried her back to her house, and Doc Barton checked in on her every day. After a while, he noticed that she wasn't aging like the rest of us. She looked as old as she did when she tried to take the rose from Miss Elaine's grave.

And, by the way, none of us every called her Snoozing Doozie back then. She was always Miss Celestine Hatton to us. Of course, no tourist is going to stop at a Miss Celestine Hatton house.

The years passed, and one day Doc Barton died. Nothing to tell about it; he just died in his sleep. We buried him, and that night there was a windstorm. Now, there had been storms since Celestine had fallen asleep, and nothing had happened. This time, though, we woke up in the morning and saw that the wind had blown down the tallest thorns. That had never happened before.

We stood on Main Street and flapped our jaws. What did it mean? Hector realized that Doc Barton had been the last person who had actually known Mr. James and Miss Elaine. All the rest of us were too young or unimportant to be involved in their feud.

You never saw folks as excited as us then. We felt sure that Miss Elaine's curse was ending. We ran up to that wall of thorns and saw that instead of being green and alive, like it had been only the day before, it was black and dead and brittle.

Hector and I felt sure that we could cut ourselves out. Some idiots wanted to burn the thorns, but Hector pointed out that the fire might burn the town down as well. So we decided to cut our way out.

Of course, those idiots who wanted to burn their way out are the ones running the Snoozing Doozie house now. Don't even try to look for a picture of Hector in there.

Hector said that if we all worked together on one part of the thorn wall, we could cut through faster. He decided we should cut along the Weston Road, figuring that once it was clear, traffic could get to us. Everybody agreed it was the thing to do, and we started to chop. Men tore into that wall with axes and clippers, and women carried the cuttings away.

Everybody was happy. Like morons, we thought we had beaten the thing, beaten Miss Elaine's curse, and all our problems were over. What a bunch of fools!

Hector worked us in shifts. A gang would cut for several hours, then rest while the next gang took over. My gang was just getting back tow work when we heard a voice from the outside.

We nearly went crazy. Somebody from the outside! Do you know how long it had been since we had seen anyone from outside Hattonville? We were so excited, we didn't pay any attention to the fact that we couldn't understand what the voice was saying.

We just cut faster and cleared the road.

Did you hear what I said? *We* cleared the road. Now, when you go to that Snoozing Doozie house, they show you that movie in which True Love or something parts the thorns for the singer. It makes me want to puke. Hard work opened up those thorns.

So anyway, we cleared the thorns, and what's the first thing we see? We see the ugliest car anyone could ever imagine. And, yes, you can see it up at the museum. It didn't even look real. It didn't have running boards, and the damn thing was pink. It was huge, bigger than any car I've ever seen, with these damn silly fins sticking up on its back like it was some kind of fish. Foolishness.

Then the driver got out. He was a handsome enough young man, but I thought his sideburns were too damn long. He had gooey stuff in his hair, and when he wasn't talking, his mouth just sneered. Five seconds after I saw him, I knew he was trouble.

"Yo, daddy," he said to me, "what's going on?"

Well, I tried to tell him, and Hector tried to tell him, and the idiots tried to tell him, and he just got bored and waved us aside. He got back behind the wheel of his ugly car and asked if he could turn around up ahead, and then some idiot mentioned Celestine and how she had been asleep since the whole thorn business started.

The young man just sneered at us.

"That's some crazy fairy tale, man," he said.

That did it. As much as I wanted him to get the hell out of my town and never come back, I couldn't stand the way he just dismissed Celestine and our whole ordeal as if it weren't even real.

"She's real, and we'll show you," I said.

We led him to the Hatton house like we were a parade. He stopped and got out of his car, leaving it running as if he thought what we would show him was only worth a glance, and followed us into the house.

Celestine lay there, on her bed, like a life-sized porcelain doll. It reminded me of the one she had broke all those years ago. Her skin was pale and flawless, and her hair was as black as a raven's wing.

"Wow, what a Snoozing Doozie," the guy sneered, and he kissed her just like that.

My jaw hit the ground at that point. I was just about to ask him who the hell he thought he was, kissing Miss Celestine like that when she had never even seen him, but then she woke up and looked him straight in the eyes.

"Hello, baby," he said.

And she grabbed him and kissed him with all her might.

I looked at that and was glad that Mr. James was dead. I walked out of the Hatton house in disgust, only to see that more people had come to Hattonville. Reporters and suchlike.

"Where's Enver Peters?" they asked.

"Who's Enver Peterrs?" I asked.

They laughed.

"Start living in the Twentieth Century, old-timer! Him, the guy who drove the pink car!"

I pointed back at the Celestine house.

"In there," I said.

They rushed past me, and the legend of Celestine and Enver Peters took wing. The reporters had great fun with us. Like it was our fault that we didn't know who Enver Peters was. We hadn't gotten radio for years, and none of us had ever heard of television, which they all found hysterically funny.

Apparently, Enver Peters had been on some big TV show and had gotten made because they wouldn't photograph him from the waist down. Hell, I wouldn't have photographed him from the waist up, because all he did with that face of his was sneer. Anyway, he had left the TV studio and driven off into the countryside, gotten lost, and found the road to Hattonville.

Headlines went out "Sleeping Town Awakened by Rock-and-Roll Singer." That's the way the country first heard the story, and that's the way Celestine wrote it up in her book, Snoozing Doozie My Story.

What did she know about it anyway? She was asleep the whole time.

Miss Celestine left with Peters that day. She never came back to Hattonville. Sure, she sent the money to start up the Snoozing Doozie House, but that's not the same.

She left and the Feds came. Nobody had paid income tax since the Depression started. Nobody had paid Social Security ever. Nobody had signed up for the Draft. No mail had been delivered. You can bet that Uncle Sam was pretty unhappy with us.

That's why we started the Snoozing Doozie house. We had to raise money or go to jail. Hector was the first to have the idea of getting tourist money, and he started the house, but he made the mistake of telling the truth. Tourists didn't like it. Doc Barton meant nothing to them. They already knew everything there was to know about Celestine, or at least they thought they did. So they threw Hector off the Board of Directors, and the town gave the tourists what they wanted. The money started pouring in, and Uncle Sam got off our backs.

Hector? He moved to Weston after that. Died.

Celestine died too, as did Enver. Some people say Enver's still alive, but those are the people dumb enough to believe the museum. I'm the only one left who knows the whole story.

What do you mean, I don't know the whole story? You're not going to read to me from that biography of Enver, are you?

Of course I haven't read it. I don't read things that will just make me mad.

Wait? What was that?

Enver Peters was Elmo Peters grandson? Our Elmo Peters, the clerk who ran off in Aught-Seven? The man Miss Elaine and Mr. James both hated? His grandson married Celestine?

Mister, you just made my day.

A Regular Day – No Peanuts

You buy a newspaper while you wait for the train and see that the flying saucers are the headline story for the third day in a row. You sigh and fold the paper under your arm. How can people be so stupid? Men from Mars indeed. You'd think people would have gotten over that Orson Welles stuff some twenty years later.

But your fellow commuters are all agog with flying saucers and little green men. The train pulls in and you settle into a seat, taking refuge in the crossword. You get the first three across and the first down, but then your attention shifts back to Ellen and how cool she was to you when she saw you off this morning. You realize she's been cool to you for a while now.

As you wonder why your marriage isn't fun anymore, the train comes to your stop. You get off and look at the time, wondering if Miss Watson is in the office. You know she has to be. Perfect, efficient, humorless Miss Watson. She could have been designed by a machine.

She showed up two weeks ago with the highest recommendations, and her typing was flawless. So you hired her. Her performance has been superb, and you've regretted hiring her ever since. She makes the office tick like a huge, lifeless clock.

You reach the Tobey Building and see Al waiting for the upper floor elevators. An idea starts taking shape between your ears. Al's always complaining about his secretary, who can barely type her way out of a wet paper bag. Why not bring him into the office to see Miss Watson? He'll snap her up, and work can be fun again.

You walk over to Al, put your arm around his shoulder and bombard him with questions about his family, as if you really cared. By the time the elevator door opens, you've steered into the subject of work, and when the elevator starts its climb, you're singing the praises of Miss Watson, the most efficient secretary you've ever had the pleasure to meet.

As the elevator passes the fifteenth floor, you admit that Miss Watson isn't happy in her job. She wants a boss who's a real striver, like Al, rather than an easy-going type like Roger O. Thornwood. By the time the door opens on the 25th Floor, Al is asking if he can stop by your office and meet Miss Watson for himself.

"You're not going to steal her away from me, are you?" you ask, all wide-eyed innocence.

Al gives you a smug smile.

"The race, Roger, is to the swiftest," he says, and you know he has swallowed the bait.

Al opens the door to your office, and a green light shines out, melting his head away.

As what's left of Al falls to the floor, you see Miss Watson standing there looking surprised. A silver ray gun sparkles in her hands. She had meant to kill you, but Al had opened the door instead. Over her shoulder, you see a weird egg-like metal contraption in the window sill as it sends a green beacon into the air.

A landing signal, you think, as you swing your briefcase into Miss Watson's chin. She falls back and releases the ray gun. You grab it and aim it at her as she hisses at you.

You try to squeeze the trigger, only to discover that there is no trigger. Meanwhile, Miss Watson's perfect face splits apart, revealing a green, reptilian visage that spits pure hatred.

You rush out of the office, still holding the ray gun. It feels soft in your hand, as if it were trying to melt or dissolve. You want to throw the alien thing away, but those old paratrooper instincts make you hold on to the weapon.

Screams come from Accounting. Flashes of green light shine out from underneath closed doors.

Suddenly you notice a red flashing light on top of your ray gun. It doesn't feel squishy in your hand anymore. In fact, the ray gun is now perfectly configured to your grip.

The door to Accounting flies open, and a reptile man steps out. You aim the ray gun at him, and a green light flashes out from your weapon. He shrieks and spasms as he melts away.

A sharp, high-pitched whistle stabs your ears. Another whistle, and then another answer it. You think it must be the reptile men talking to each other, and by the time you've identified five different whistles, you decide to get the hell out.

To get to the stairway, you have to go by Accounting. You send a blast from the ray gun through the doorway. Enraged whistles shriek, and you feel satisfaction.

You hit the stairway door and start down the steps, taking them two, sometimes three, at a time. You ask yourself some questions, like how many of these reptilian things are there, and how soon will your ray gun run out of whatever it shoots?

Footsteps echo from above you and below. Are there reptile creatures behind you or people? You decide to keep going down, get out of the building.

Turning a corner, you come across a knot of baffled women and men.

"Keep moving," you say. "We have to get out of here."

In a daze, they start down the stairs, hardly as fast as you'd like. The door to the next landing opens, and a scaly head peaks through. You aim and fire, but not before the creature emits a loud whistle. Its head melts away, and when you look around for your people, you see that they're two flights below you and picking up speed.

You catch up and are in the rear of the group when they reach the door to the main lobby. No reptile creatures in the lobby, only shocked people and half-melted bodies. You hurry over to the glass door to Arnold Avenue and look out. Reptiles are standing on the sidewalk, pointing up at the sky.

You go through the revolving door and zap the nearest lizard. He hasn't fully melted when you zap the second one. Creature number three has drawn his ray gun but when he sees his melted friends, he drops his weapon and runs.

Just before you fire at him, a shadow passes overhead, and you have to look up.

It's a flying saucer, a goddam flying saucer, perfectly round, with strange red lights flashing around its edge in a nearly hypnotic way. It stops in the air, and an opening dilates at the bottom, letting a shimmering ladder emerge.

You shoot the ladder, which glows and twists but doesn't melt. Taller reptile creatures, carrying big ray guns that take two hands, trot down the ladder, jumping past the section you hit, and land on the pavement with an undignified thump.

As the third one hits the ground and starts to straighten up, a green ray fired from behind you hits him and he melts.

Spurred back into action, you fire and burn away the first tall reptile creature. You and your unknown ally finish off the second, as the flying saucer retreats and turns down the next street to disgorge its load in safety.

You turn to see who helped you, and you're stunned to see it's a woman.

She's a tall redhead, maybe in her forties. Her hair's cut short, and she wears a black blouse and tan skirt with a colorful peasant-style scarf around her neck. Of course, she's carrying a ray gun. You haven't seen many women like her before.

"Who are you?" you ask.

"Rorey," she says. "Aurora Higgins. My friends call me Rorey."

"Roger Thornwood," you say.

"I came down here bringing a painting I sold," she says. "And I ran into this."

You look at her and think how unlike Ellen she is and how unlike Miss Watson she is, and then you remember Miss Watson and those other reptile things in the Tobey Building. You throw yourself into Rorey and knock her off the sidewalk just before a green ray shoots out from the building and melts the sidewalk where you two were standing.

"What do we do next?" Rorey askes as she fires at the Tobey Building, melting the revolving door. "Go after that saucer?"

You look at the sky. Might there be more saucers? What can the two of you do against so many creatures anyway?

Then you look at Rorey. You shrug.

"It's the only plan we have," you say.

"My taxi's still running," she says. "It's over there." She points and then blasts a reptile face in a window. "I was paying the driver when the saucer flew up, and he jumped out of the car and ran away."

The two of you run over to the yellow vehicle. You get in the driver's seat, while she keeps up a covering fire. You turn down an alley parallel to the flying saucer's path and speed along like a mad devil.

Just as you reach Corman Street, a reptile creature walks in front of the alley. You suppress your instinct to break and slam the cab into him. He shatters, spraying green stuff everywhere, but his two-handed ray rifle skitters along the pavement. Now you stop the cab.

You and Rorey leap from the taxi just before a green ray melts it. You grab the ray rifle, and its goes soft in your hands, but Rorey shoots the nearest reptile creature.

She takes out a second one and then a third. The creatures see that you have a rifle, and they sure as hell don't want you to use it. Whistling like mad teapots, they charge across the street at you two, but you feel the weapon configuring in your hands.

You aim at the nearest one and put a green ray into his face just above that whistling, ululating mouth.

The surviving people scattered along the sidewalk cheer as the creature's head inflates to twice its size and then explodes.

Turning, you see the flying saucer. You aim at the ladder and fire. The ladder shimmers and twists over on itself, trapping those reptile creatures trying to disembark. You fire again at the ladder, and the thing breaks free from the saucer and crashes to the ground. The saucer itself now starts dipping from side to side.

The reptile creatures on the ground now look up at the saucer. Their whistling takes on a new tone. You swear it sounds worried.

The opening at the bottom of the saucer tried to dilate shut, but it remains half-open. The reptile creatures now run after the saucer, like they're afraid of being left behind here.

With Rorey standing next to you, you aim at the opening in the saucer and fire.

The flashing red lights around the rim of the flying saucer go out. The reptilian whistling reaches a note of hysteria, and the saucer, as if the string holding it up in the air has been cut, falls to Corman Avenue, lands on its rim, rolls for a block, and then turns bright blue before crumbling into dust.

The reptile creatures start to shake. Their weapons fall from their hands, and they run into the pile of blue dust, whistling madly. People pick up the alien weapons and within moments start blasting down the reptiles, but you find your arm around Rorey's waist. Her arms is around yours, and the next thing you know, you're kissing her.

"Show me this wonderful painting of yours," you say after a while.

As the two of you walk back to the cab, a new shadow appears over the city. You look up and see a huge flying saucer, maybe twelve times the size of the first. From its underside comes a yellow ray that widens out to cover the whole of the city.

As you and Rorey start to run, everything around you, including Rorey herself, becomes snowy, like bad reception on a television set.

You shake your head and give a dime to the guy at the newspaper stand. You read the paper as you wait for your train and see that Sputnik is the headline story for the third day in a row. You get on the train and think about how chilly your marriage to Ellen has become. At the Tobey Building, you ride the elevator up with Al, and you commiserate with him about inefficient secretaries. Yours, Miss Morrison, is always losing things.

During your lunch hour, you pass a striking redhead, an arty type, carrying a package that you assume must be a painting. You notice her, and something about her tickles your memory, but try as you might, you don't remember her, so you walk by without saying anything.

When you get home, Ellen gives you a perfunctory peck on the cheek.

"How was your day?" she asks.

"Fine," you say, "just a regular day like all the rest."

Even as the words come out of your mouth, you know that isn't exactly right. Something happened today, something unusual, but damned if you can remember what it is now. It's just a memory you can't get hold of.

That night, you kiss Ellen as she lies there next to you. For some reason, that arty redhead from your lunch hour pops into your head. You can't imagine why you would think of her now.

You put your head on your pillow and fall asleep, and the redhead is gone.

"So can I get you come coffee?" I asked as Bill sat down in my family room.

"No thanks. You got some pop?"

"Sure," I said. Then I remembered something from the last time Bill visited. "It's diet."

"Oh." His face fell. "Look, I'll just have water then."

"Okay." I went out to the kitchen, opened a bottle of Evian, and divided it equally between two glasses.

It was a pain having Bill over. Thank God he lived out of state. He visited his Mom twice a year. What a depressing chore that must be. So he wanted to visit an old friend as a break from that grimness. It was okay with me, although Debbie couldn't stand him.

"He's a loser," she'd say. "He looks like one. Talks like one. If you hang around him too long, it'll rub off on you too."

So I always tried to schedule Bill's visits for evenings when Debbie took the kids out. She never saw him, and it saved me from hearing her dissect everything Bill said for personality flaws for the next three days.

"Here you go," I said, giving him the glass. "How's life treating you these days?"

"The usual." He shrugged "I'm not really interested in 'these days,' not since Ann left me."

"Yeah, well." I nodded. The divorce had been a real body blow to Bill, the only one who hadn't seen it coming.

"I'm more interested in the old days," Bill said.

I suppressed a groan. That meant Faith Elementary, which was longer ago than I cared to remember. Adult men weren't supposed to go around thinking that their best days were before they could shave. Debbie was right. This guy was a loser.

I laughed. "Hell, I'm lucky if I can remember my daughter's years in primary school."

"I need to talk to you about this, Frank." Bill looked at me, and I could tell he was utterly serious. "I almost think I'm going crazy, and I need you to help me."

I spread my hands.

"I'm happy to help. Only my memory isn't too good."

Bill stood up and looked out the window. Snow swirled past the streetlight.

"Third grade," he said. "We had Mr. Torgerson that year."

I smiled automatically.

"Big redheaded guy. The first male teacher we had."

"That's right. It was also the first year we were in a room with older kids."

Back then, Faith Elementary put its upper grades in the same rooms: Third Grade with Fourth, Fifth Grade with Sixth, and Seventh Grade with Eighth. It was hell for the odd-grade kids, particularly one without an older brother, like Bill.

"You had a rough year of it," I said at last.

"I hated it. I was never so glad to see Christmas come and get those two weeks off from school."

The wind outside lashed the wires and made the snow dance.

"Do you remember that Christmas vacation?"

"No," I said.

"Not at all?"

I shrugged. "They all run together for me."

Bill sat down and looked at me, his eyes bright with enthusiasm.

"Think back. I had forgotten it, forgotten it for years, when I just remembered a few days ago."

"What am I supposed to remember?"

"It snowed."

"It snows every December."

Bill looked like he wanted to shake my shoulders.

"A big snow. They actually started vacation a day early, the first time they ever did that. Remember?"

A memory tickled. It sounded right, but I kept a poker face.

"Everything was shut down," Bill said. "My mom had gone downtown to work, and she got stuck there overnight. My grandpa didn't know what to do with me, so he sent me outside to play."

How could I know any of this, I wondered, but Bill wasn't even seeing me anymore. His eyes were on an eight-year-old kid pulling a sled off into a white, winter adventure.

"I sledded down Elm Hill road. They closed the road. It was great." He grinned, and I felt happy for him.

"The next day, the roads were clear. Your mom called and asked if Chuck could take us over to the park."

Chuck had just gotten his license that winter, I remembered. He would drive anywhere, anytime, just to be behind the wheel.

"He drove us out to the park. It looked like a million kids were there on the sled run. We had to stand in line to go down the hill, and when I went down, some big kids on a toboggan crashed into me and sent me flying. My nose bled, and I stopped it with my scarf."

God yes, Bill had looked ridiculous standing there, crying, holding his scarf to his nose. I didn't even want to admit that I knew him, but I asked if he were okay.

"I don't want to sled anymore!"

The kids who had hit him laughed.

"Look, we just got here," I told him. "I don't want to ask Chuck to take us home now. He'll think we're babies."

"Well, I'm not going to sled."

"Fine." I picked up my sled and turned to start back up the hill. "Do something else. Make a snowman."

I blinked and looked at the excited middle-aged man standing before me. Why didn't Bill remember how I acted that day? Was he trying to be nice? I could feel myself begin to get angry.

"I was lucky," Bill said. "I found a place where some kids had made a good start on a snowman. All he needed was a head. Usually I had rotten luck making my snowmen, but this time I put the head together like a pro. I got it up on that torso, and I found some newly broken branches for arms."

Bill smiled at the memory.

"I looked at that guy, and I thought he looked kinda empty, I guess, so I wrapped my scarf around his neck, and he came to life."

"What?"

"My snowman came to life. It must have been my blood on the scarf. I've thought about it a lot lately. You see, I gave him my blood, and he came to life."

I couldn't talk for a moment. Finally, I opened my mouth.

"Bill, snowmen do not come to life. This is reality, not some stupid Christmas special."

"Frank, the snowman came to life, and you saw him."

"The hell I did."

"Yes you did. You came back into the woods to find me, and you saw me with my snowman."

"I did not."

Bill laughed.

"Hey, I understand. We were so scared about this that we didn't tell anybody. We didn't even talk about it between ourselves. You ran away when you saw my snowman move."

Oh-ho, I thought, he was casting *me* as the coward in his fantasy.

"Your snowman came to life, and you've kept it secret for all these years?"

"I've repressed it." Bill paced. "I only remembered it last week. Yes, I was listening to 'Frosty the Snowman' on the radio. I was writing a Christmas card to Ann and Mike and Lisa." He took a deep breath. "I wondered if anything magical had ever happened in my life, and then I remembered my snowman."

He beamed.

"Don't you see, Frank? If it happened once, it can happen again. Not a magic snowman this time, but something magical. Maybe it can bring my family back together again."

I stood up. "Your snowman never came to life. You got hit by a toboggan, went into the woods to make a snowman, and imagined it came to life. Imagined."

He stared at me as if I were speaking in Greek.

"I never saw a magic snowman," I said. "I saw a confused kid with a bloody nose."

Bill took a step back from me. "That's not true. You saw the snowman dance with me, and you screamed and ran away. I ran after you to tell you that it was all right, that he was my friend. When I brought you back to the clearing, the snowman was gone, but he left my scarf on a tree branch."

"Why are you making me the coward in this fantasy? It's bad enough I have to listen to this nonsense, but you have to make me the coward who runs away!" I was hot.

"But you did."

"I did not! I didn't even see a snowman!"

"You did!"

I turned my back on him. "I can't even believe we have to talk about this. Snowmen don't come to life. There's no such thing as magic."

He didn't say anything, so I turned around to look at his sad face. "That's the reason Ann left you. You're just a big silly kid who can't grow up."

Bill looked like he did when the toboggan hit him. He turned and walked over to get his coat. I opened the door without a word. Snowflakes rushed inside.

He walked out, not looking at me. I stood in the doorway, watching the snow swirl past and wondered if Debbie would be safe driving home. As Bill pulled out of the driveway, his headlights illuminated a snowman the neighbor kids had built.

I watched the light move across the whiteness and remembered how huge the snow-covered evergreens in McKinley Park had looked that day. Bill's laugh, from a happy eight-year-old's throat, rang again in my ears, and it was joined by another laugh, one that sounded like wind over a chimney on a cold December night.

I shut my eyes and once again saw a delighted Bill standing there in the frozen clearing, a jolly snowman dancing around him.

I opened my eyes and grit my teeth. Why had it been his snowman that came to life instead of any of mine?

Kiss

He hopped to the edge of the pool and searched the sky for storks. The horrible birds had been about Clotilda's garden earlier this week, forcing him to remain below water and away from the grass far more than he would have liked.

Something important was going on at the palace. The robins sang of nothing but the two princely retinues that arrived earlier, and the water beetles eagerly spread the news.

He disliked the two princes. Clotilda's father must be pressuring her to marry soon. The idea made his huge white throat bulge with anger. Clotilda was his. She had been made by Fate for him. A kiss from her, and his miserable froggish state, this tiresome crouching in murky water and eating flies, would end. He had to get to her before the interloping princes prevailed over her good sense.

It had been only a few weeks since he had come to the realization that he was not really a frog at all. True, he had no memories of life before being a frog, but the pond had always seemed small to him, its depths a prison and not a place of safety. However, his froggishness had always seemed an inescapable fact of nature, and he could see no way out of it, although the odor of water lilies offended, and the taste of flies seemed a necessity and never a pleasure.

Then, one day, Clotilda's cousins, the Duke of Tarboard and his sister, played in the garden by the pond. The Duke, a spirited brat of nine summers, after harassing his sister by singing, with more enthusiasm than skill, all sixteen verses of "The Troll Changeling Bridegroom," received a kick in the hindquarters that sent him into the lily-covered pond. The unquenchable lad had sprung to his feet, waving one of the frogs of the pond in his grasp.

"Here's a bridegroom for you, Deirdre! Kiss him and make him a handsome prince!"

Deirdre placed her hands on her brother's forehead and shoved him back into the pond.

Fortunately, he had not been the frog in the Duke's hands, but he had heard all that had been said. The words fired his interest. They had to explain why he disliked the pond and his fellows so much.

Before sunset, he talked to a robin, who put him in touch with a starling who sang outside the palace windows.

"Oh, yes," the starling had said. "It's little Deirdre's favorite story, it is, about the frog prince. Her nurse tells her about it every day."

"Tell me."

She told him as best she could, which was not at all well, starlings being most interested in themselves and tending to ignore other creatures. He got the idea, though. A handsome prince was turned into a frog by an evil witch and then restored to his true state by the kiss of a beautiful princess.

As the starling twittered through the story, his life suddenly made sense to him. No wonder he differed from his fellows in the pond. He had nothing in common with them save his outward appearance, which was clearly false and imposed on him by some malign force. Just one kiss would reveal his true self.

At that instance, the face of Clotilda – elegant pale skin, rich copper hair, and bright green eyes – appeared in his mind. He knew that she was the princess meant to break his spell.

He knew it, but Clotilda did not. How he wished the silly starling had told him *how* the princess had met the frog. He had never been to the palace, and while Clotilda strolled through the garden at times, she did not do so as frequently as in earlier years. Worse, she hardly came to the edge of the pond, and he feared moving too far from the edge of the water lest the storks see him.

Yesterday, however, the servants had done something odd. They came to the flat ground by the pond and pounded wooden stakes and things that looked like thin horseshoes into the ground. They followed the very precise directions of the major domo, who paced off the distance between the horseshoes and made the servants move them around until he was satisfied.

Watching the activity made his chest pound with anticipation. Clotilda must have ordered this peculiar construction, and he knew that it would bring her to him.

The flap of wings made him leap back into the water.

Curse the stork, he thought.

He through of Clotilda and swam to the surface. His courage received instant reward, for Clotilda strode across the field toward him.

Her red hair fell past her shoulders, which were covered by a dress of light blue. She held a mallet in her hands and swung it energetically, laughing as the two princes followed her.

The first, a handsome man with coal-black hair and elegantly trimmed beard, sported a blue-and-white jacket with a ruffled collar. Holding his mallet with one hand, so that its head hung toward the ground, he gave the impression of wishing he could leave it someplace unremarked.

As tall as he was, the second prince loomed even taller, trudging across the field with his mallet resting on his shoulder. Clean-shaved with bright blond hair, this prince scowled at the first and gripped his mallet whenever the first prince spoke or laughed. He wore a red jacket and peculiar leather shorts.

"I am sure you are both familiar with this game," Clotilda said. "Are you, Prince Etienne?"

"Most assuredly," the first prince said. He smiled and bowed to Clotilda.

"And you, Prince Arnulf?"

"I am with the game not familiar," the second prince said.

The first prince winked at Clotilda. She winked back and then frowned briefly at the loud croaking that came from the pond.

"Dear Prince Arnulf, I am sorry that this game has not penetrated your homeland. Still, it is quite simple to learn, and you shall learn by playing."

Arnulf raised the mallet from his shoulder, looked at its wooden head, and then looked at the first prince's smiling countenance.

"I look forward to it." Arnulf's lips pulled tight and revealed his teeth.

Clotilda laughed, a bright, musical laugh, and, in the pond, he nearly swooned for joy. His chest puffed in and out as Clotilda explained the rules of the game and the order of play. Arnulf should go first, followed by Etienne, with herself last. As she talked, her gorgeous, thin lips captivated him, and he hopped from lily pad to lily pad.

"Beastly frog," Etienne said, looking at him.

"Pray go first, Prince Arnulf," Clotilda said.

The burly prince walked to the end of the field, where two hoops stood before a stake. He placed his red ball the length of a mallet head from the stake and then swung the mallet into the ball with all his might.

The two hoops caught on his mallet and flew into the air, while the ball sped across the garden, past the opposite stake. Clotilda and Etienne laughed. Not wishing to be excluded, he croaked loudly from his seat on the lily pad.

"Dear Prince Arnulf," Clotilda said, wiping tears of mirth from her eyes. "This is not a battlefield. One only needs to tap the ball and use one's wits."

"I am so happy to have made you laugh, dear Clotilda." Arnulf bent over and shoved the hoops back into the ground with great force. "So very, very happy. This game is not played in my homeland."

"Get your ball and play after fair Clotilda," Etienne said, setting up his orange ball. "After seeing my turn and the princess' you will have some idea how to play."

On the lily pad, he shifted and paid close attention. After the kiss, as a prince he assumed he would need knowledge of this game.

Etienne nearly tapped his ball through the first two hoops. Then he sent it toward a hoop to the right. He bowed to Prince Arnulf after he reached the ball, then bent to strike it through the hoop. Unfortunately, it hit one of the hoop's arms and sprang back.

Etienne nodded, satisfied at its lay for his next shot.

Clotilda rushed into play, sending her yellow ball through the first hoops and taking her second shot before the princes could compliment her.

Her ball rolled not toward the hoop but straight at Etienne's ball. They met with a wooden thunk. Etienne blinked but kept a serene countenance.

Clotilda brandished her mallet as she strode over to where the balls lay and firmly planted her foot on the yellow.

Etienne ran his finger around his ruffled collar. "Croquet can be a friendly game."

Clotilda looked at him, measured his distress, then swung the mallet into her ball, sending Etienne's flying a good six feet away.

On the lily pad, he croaked in triumph, while Prince Arnulf brayed.

"It can be friendly, Prince Etienne," Clotilda said, "when it is played among friends." She drove her ball through the third hoop and toward the center hoop. "You and Arnulf are hardly friends. You are rivals for my hand."

As she stepped forward to swing, Arnulf spoke. "When do I play again?"

"Never."

Clotilda shot her ball through the center hoop. "I've read all the ambassador's reports on your fine homeland, dear prince, and I have no intention of living in a country where all the palaces are drafty and under heated, the chief meal is potatoes, and the only entertainment is watching the mechanical clock figures move every hour."

He croaked with relief on the pad. He had thought the bigger prince was a formidable rival, but now he could tell that Arnulf would never win Clotilda. He leaped into the pond and dived to the bottom to say farewell to its depths.

As he broke the surface, Clotilda's ball struck the far stake, and now the princess began her way back.

"And as for you, dear Etienne, have they cured your pox yet?"

Etienne's mouth opened, but no sound came out, at least none that could be heard over the croaking of a frog.

"There are perfectly sensible reasons of state for denying the both of you." Clotilda played on. "If I marry Arnulf, my kingdom shall probably get dragged into his father's great way, and Daddy is surrounded by three very large enemies, is he not?"

"The more foes, the greater the glory," the blond prince said.

Clotilda shrugged. "I prefer not to have my palace burned down around my ears, thank you very much. And if I marry Etienne, the merchants of his kingdom will no doubt demand access to our sugar islands."

As the two princes stood silent, she tapped her ball through the final two hoops and into the original stake.

"I win," she said.

Etienne bowed slightly.

"Clearly, you have superior skill at croquet." He stroked his thin moustache. "I think that we had as much chance at winning your hand as we had at winning this game."

"Less, actually," Clotilda said. "The idea that I would wed either of you…"

Now was his moment. He knew it was so. He hopped and he hooped until, at last, he landed on the princess' shoe.

Clotilda looked down at him. He looked up at her beauty and loved her fine red hair and dazzling green eyes, her effortless skill at beating these two princes, and her bravery. Now was his moment. The curse would be lifted.

"The idea that I would wed either of you is more preposterous than the idea that I should wed this frog."

So saying, she swept him up from her foot, raised him to her face, and kissed him.

"Abominable!" Etienne declared.

"Wretchedness!" Arnulf snapped the mallet's handle and threw both pieces into the pond.

The foreign princes turned their back on Clotilda and began walking back to the palace.

Meanwhile, he squirmed in Clotilda's hand, waiting for the bolt of magic that would liberate him from his false frog state. Her breath warmed him, and he thought his skin dried a bit. He closed his eyes and shook with anticipation, awaiting his transformation, but when he opened them, he saw that he remained a frog.

Clotilda dropped him to the ground and laughed.

"How foolish these princes are. Good riddance to them."

Oblivious to the hopping and croaking near her feet, the princess danced around her field of victory.

How could the magic not work? he wondered. When a princess kissed an enchanted frog, the frog always changed back to being a prince. She had kissed him, but….

Perhaps she were not a true princess but a troll changeling left in her place? He croaked loudly. Yes, she couldn't be a real princess, only a troll.

He leaped onto her shoe again, croaking loudly, trying to warn everyone, Etienne, Arnulf, the servants, that this was no princess but a troll.

None paid heed to him.

Clotilda must be a changeling, he told himself, for if she were a true princess, that could only mean he was a….

"Vile thing," Clotilda said, and she shook him off her foot and walked toward the palace.

… a frog who dreamed he was a prince.

He squatted in the middle of the croquet field. Vile – that he was. A vile, puffed-up fool to think that a princess' kiss would release him from the frogishness that was his birthright.

He was a frog. The pond was his true home.

He could not move as the idea weighed down on him.

Part of his brain warned of danger, screamed that he was too far from the pond, cried that even now a stork must be flying toward him.

But part of his brain told him that if the kiss of a princess could not end his frog existence, the kiss of a stork surely could.

A Day for Douglas Ford

The first rays of sunlight caught the painters finishing up atop the water tower. They lowered their gear to the ground and prepared to go home and sleep as the alarm clock rang in Douglas Ford's bedroom.

Douglas Ford moaned and sat up. Barbara turned over and whispered in his ear.

"A few more minutes."

"Sure."

Douglas sat on the edge of the bed, looked at his toes, and reviewed what had to be done at the bank today. He peeked out the window and noticed the bright blue sky, highlighted by wisps of cirrus clouds.

Just the kind I like, he thought, and hurried off to the bathroom to shave and shower. Barbara was up when he came out, and he dressed while she washed. Once decent, he headed outside for the paper.

It was his favorite kind of sky, he marveled, as he walked down the driveway to the yellow, plastic <u>Tribune</u> box. He pulled the paper out and automatically ripped the plastic bag off the newspaper without bothering to look at the headlines as he walked back to the house. The paper felt light, and he remembered that Thursday always seemed like a dull day for the <u>Trib</u>.

He dropped the paper on the table and started the coffeemaker so it would be ready when Barbara came out. She never talked much before her coffee.

Doug spun the paper around so he could read the headlines.

DOUGLAS FORD DAY, the newspaper proclaimed.

"Oh, my God," he said.

He covered the entire front page above the fold. On the left were four pictures – baby picture, high school graduation picture, wedding picture, and a picture that must have been taken yesterday of him mowing the lawn. On the right was a detailed appreciation of his life.

"Douglas Ford," the article said, "is one of those people whose simple, unassuming dignity is a well-recognized feature of life in Punderson. He does his work, raises his family, and all who meet him know that it is through men like Douglas Ford that Punderson is a fine place to live and America is a great nation."

Then it went on to cover his birth in the town hospital.

Barbara walked into the kitchen and poured a coup of coffee.

"Have you ever seen anything like this?" Doug asked.

"Like what?"

He held the front page out to her. Her eyes widened as she realized what she was reading.

"Oh, my God! Doug, this is incredible!"

"Is it a joke?" he asked.
Barbara head the front page and turned to the continuation on page 3. She shook her head.

"No. It's just straightforward reporting, as far as I can tell."

The phone rang as Kim, her eyes barely open, entered the kitchen.

"What's up, Dad?"

He shook his head as Barbara answered the phone.

"It's Wilson, editor of the <u>Tribune</u>," she said.

Doug took the phone.

"Mr. Ford, sir?" the editor asked. "I hope you're pleased with the article.

"I am. It's a very big surprise."

"Well, it wouldn't have worked if it weren't a surprise, would it? You would have posed for that picture. Instead we have a real shot of a decent American doing an everyday American task. It would probably win a Pulitzer, if I had my way."

"I'm sure it will."

"Well, just so you're pleased, Mr. Ford. You're one of the people who makes this country great. I'll be watching <u>Biography</u> tonight to see how they handle your story."

After Wilson had hung up, Doug still held the phone to his ear. *It must be a joke*, he thought. <u>Biography</u>? It couldn't be possible. Where had they hidden the cameras?

The doorbell rang.

"I'll get it," Kim said, running out of the kitchen.

"Is your father at home?" a familiar voice asked.

Doug hung up and tried to place that voice when Mayor Sweeney walked in, sporting his customary red bow tie and a broad smile.

"Congratulations, Douglas," he said, unaware that his voice was too loud for the kitchen. "I've proclaimed today Douglas Ford Day, and I have to say that Punderson has never been so proud." He worked Doug's hand like a pump then looked at Barbara.

"The parade kicks off at 1 PM sharp. You'll have him in something decent by then, won't you?" Mayor Sweeney cast a quick glance over Doug's morning attire. "The networks will all be there. CNN is outside now. This might be okay for them, but the networks *are* the networks."

Barbara beamed, saved Doug's hand from the Mayor, and kissed her husband's cheek.

"We'll be fine."

"Good. Come with me, Douglas." The Mayor beckoned. "I have a surprise for you."

A surprise? Doug wondered. The whole day had been nothing but surprises.

He let Sweeney lead him out of the house. Sure enough, CNN was in the front yard. It was that guy who did all the heartland stories for them. Usually when he came on, Doug picked up the TV Guide.

"What's it like, Mr. Ford?" the guy asked.

"Nothing like it." Douglas shrugged as the Mayor urged him forward. "Best damn day of my life."

Immediately, Doug felt guilty about saying "damn" on TV. But CNN was cable, he reminded himself, and maybe cable was easier about that kind of thing.

Mayor Sweeney opened up the limo door for Doug. After they got in and the car rolled away, Sweeney looked at Doug and started to tear up.

"It's people like you, Douglas, who have everything. A wife, a kid, a good job. This ordinary decency that makes life go on. Me, all my life I've struggled to be better than the next guy, get my picture in the paper, have the crowd at the Fourth of July picnic listen to my every word, and now I see how empty it all is. You're the real hero. I'm just a blowhard."

Tears ran down the Mayor's cheeks.

Doug didn't know what to do. He opened his mouth, but he couldn't think of what to say. Then the limo stopped, and Mayor Sweeney motioned for him to get out.

They had come to the Punderson city limit. At first, Doug looked at the acres and acres of soybeans that stretched off to the west, but then Mayor Sweeney put his hands on Doug's shoulders and directed him to the east, to the water tower.

Doug gasped. Overnight someone had painted his face on Punderson's water tower. His face beamed down, bright and serene, like the sun, blessing his neighbors with his benevolence. The artist had rendered Doug with hyper-precise clarity and gave the viewer an overwhelming desire to be loved by the subject of the painting.

Mayor Sweeney squeezed Doug's shoulders.

"Congratulations, Douglas. You deserve it."

People came out of their houses to line the streets as the limo took Doug home. He opened the moon roof, stood up, and waved. The people burst into applause.

"Way to go, Doug!"

"It couldn't happen to a nicer guy!"

Tears formed at the corners of Doug's eyes. This was *his* town. He had been born here and had gone to school here. He left for college, but he came back afterwards. For all those years, Punderson had just been the place that he lived. He always assumed his life would have been much the same if he had been born in Blufferton, or if his folks had moved to Indiana, as they had talked about doing when he was ten.

Now he knew that this wasn't so. No other town could offer him such love. No other town could let him express himself as he had and reward him for it. They needed him to show the country, the whole world, what they were like.

The limo stopped in front of Doug's house. The crowd kept a respectful distance.

"I'll be back at 12:30," the chauffeur said. "The parade kicks off at one."

A parade for me, Doug thought, walking up the driveway. My mother should have lived to see this.

"Douglas?"

He turned and saw Ann Markham, his neighbor. He had never liked her. She always acted like she was too good for Punderson, like she belonged in New York or Chicago. She always talked about the theater or how they should show foreign films in the library, or something else designed to make a person feel small.

Now she looked sorry.

"Douglas, I know we've never been especially close," she said, "but I read the article in the newspaper today, and I've seen the profiles on TV, and I realize that it's all my fault."

"Well...."

"I realize there's more to you than meets the eye. I can see that now." She dabbed her own eyes. "I was just too self-centered to realize it."

She burst into full-fledged tears.

Douglas put his arm around her.

"Hey, you weren't that bad," he said. "No damage done. Don't beat yourself up."

She gripped his hand and looked up into his face.

"Thank you," she said, before leading him into her house.

Three steps up from the door was the kitchen. A box of flesh jelly donuts lay open on the table.

"Strawberry jelly," Ann said.

"My favorite! How did you know?"

"It was part of the profile of you on <u>Good Morning America</u> today. Help yourself."

Doug picked up a donut and took a bite. He closed his eyes as its taste exceeded his expectations.

"Do you want to join me?"

"I was going to ask you the same thing," Ann said.

Doug opened his eyes and nearly choked. Ann stood nude in the hallway between the kitchen and the center hall. She looked at him without any embarrassment.

"Douglas Ford, I know you think I'm an arrogant bitch, but I do appreciate you, and this is the only way I can show you how sorry I am."

Doug had often wondered what Ann looked like naked. She was taller than Barbara and slimmer. From the way she talked and moved, he had imagined she would be a lot more active in bed than Barbara.

"Sure," he said, as he walked over to her.

Barbara had set the table for lunch when Doug got home. He didn't know what to say or how to act. Sex with Ann had been fantastic. She had real enthusiasm for oral sex and the dog style. He had actually felt a bit threatened by her enthusiasm, as if he might not keep up with her. Surely Barbara must have heard them talking, had seen him going into her house, could see the guilt on his face even now as he looked at her, he wondered.

Barbara smiled at him, kissed him on the cheek, and gripped his hand.

"Now Ann knows what a treasure I have," she said. She smiled proudly at Doug. "Her books and theater can't keep her warm at night."

Doug could hardly believe his ears.

"Eat up fast, the limo'll be here soon."

Doug barely had time to shower before the limo arrived. As it carried him to Arrowhead Park, he noticed that everyone displayed a picture of him in an least one window of their home. The Tribune had apparently published a full-sheet portrait of him, like they did with Santa in December, and a lot of Pundersonites had taped it up in their windows. Some even displayed the front page photos or even photos of Doug they had blown up themselves.

He marveled at it all. "What a town."

The high school marching band, the Pirates, began playing the theme from Rocky when he got out of the limo. The crowd cheered, roaring when Doug threw some punches and jogged in a brief circle.

"The public likes you, Douglas," Mayor Sweeney said. "You'll have my job next."

The politicians surrounded Douglas and quickly instructed him as to where he should sit, at what point he would get the key to the city, how long he could speak, and the like.

At 1 PM precisely, Mayor Sweeney signaled for the band to stop. He approached the podium and began to speak about dignity, patriotism, love of family, and all the other uniquely American virtues that were embodied in Douglas Ford.

Doug had always considered hearing Mayor Sweeney speak to be the secret cost of attending a free city-sponsored event. The man would talk a subject into the ground. To listen to him go on and on about the sacred dead of the Second World War usually made Doug wish that Sweeney were numbered among them.

Yet today, hearing Mayor Sweeney talk about him, Doug realized how right the man was. He, Douglas Ford, loved his country, had dealt fairly with people, and saved money for his family. If more people had done this, the country would be in as bad a shape as it was. His ordinary dignity was truly extraordinary today. Punderson had gotten on CNN because of him, not because some drug-crazed kid had killed his teacher.

The Mayor finished talking. Doug stood up and walked over to receive the key to the city. It was a huge, Medieval-looking thing, made of frosted glass instead of iron. It weighed enough, though, Doug decided.

He approached the microphone.

"Pundersonites, I will never forget this day. You made this possible. This key... this key will be the best thing I own."

The crowd thundered its applause. The high school band broke into some march he didn't recognize. The crowd, however, clearly knew the melody, for they broke into song:

"Everybody loves Doug Ford; he's the best."

Doug wept. It was the greatest moment of his life.

Mayor Sweeney clapped him on the back.

"Great music, huh? Mr. Caprillorio, the band director, has been working on it since we got the word last night."

Sweeney led Doug to an electric blue convertible. The band followed. Behind the band came the crowd, now holding pictures of Douglas Ford mounted on ping-pong paddles. As Doug waved at them, everyone turned their paddles around to show signs that said: "We love our Doug."

The band swung into "Stars and Stripes Forever," and the people sang:

"Hooray for Douglas Ford!! He's the man all Punderson adores!

He's good and regular and true. Douglas Ford will stand by you!

Hooray for Douglas Ford!! He's the man all Punderson adores!

We all love Douglas Ford! Oh, Douglas Ford, oh, Douglas Ford, oh, Douglas Ford!"

By the time the parade had circled back through Punderson to Arrowhead Park, Douglas Ford felt like he had been riding on a cloud.

He got out of the convertible and rushed over to Mr. Caprillorio and shook his hand.

"That was wonderful!"

"You inspired me, Mr. Ford," the band director said. "I'm so glad you liked it. I would stay up for night nights in a row, working on a song, to hear you say you liked it."

"Well, I did. I think it's great."

Caprillorio saw two drummers fooling around and ran off to restore order. Doug stood still and let out his breath. For the first time in hours, nobody was looking at him. He let his shoulders sag and twisted his head from side to side.

"We're glad you liked it."

Doug turned to look at a trio of band girls. One, a clarinet player, who was looking at him as if expecting a pearl of wisdom, captured his attention. He recognized her as Cheryl, Kim's classmate.

He had never seen Cheryl in uniform before. The royal blue highlighted her pale skin and honey-blonde hair.

"You kids did a great job," he told them.

All three glowed. Unlike Cheryl, who was as tall as Doug, the two flutists were short, petite and dark. All three seemed so bright that Doug wished that Kim had taken up an instrument like them, but instead she had just drifted through high school. He realized that his daughter would probably never have a day like this in her life.

Doug looked around. City officials had started distributing hot dogs and potato salad. Nobody was looking for him now.

"I'd like to go home and take a shower," he said. "It would be great not to be the center of attention for a while."

"I brought my dad's car," Cheryl said. "I can take you home."

"Great."

He followed her to a red Saturn. Cheryl eased the car out, past a van that had parked too close at an odd angle, and got to the street.

"You drive well," Doug said. Kim wouldn't be half this careful, he left unsaid. She probably would have dinged his car in a situation like this.

"Thanks," Cheryl said. "I have to stop at home. I still have some books that Kim leant me to read."

"Fine. I'm sure she'll be glad to get them back."

They drove to Cheryl's house, with Doug waving at the few pedestrians they saw. The teenager pulled into the driveway and turned the car off.

"Mr. Ford, I know Kim's books are in my room, but my room looks like a tornado hit it. I'll have to dig for them. If you don't mind coming inside to wait. You can talk to my mom."

Doug went inside, but Mrs. Wheeler wasn't home. A box of strawberry jelly donuts lay on the kitchen table, and he found some Diet Pepsi Free in the fridge. He had just finished the donut when Cheryl came down the stairs.

"The boys at Punderson High are really turds," he could hear her say as she approached the kitchen. "I can't take any of them seriously."

Nude, Cheryl stepped into the kitchen, her honey blonde hair spilling over her freckled shoulders.

"I find older men attractive."

Doug showered at the Wheelers', and Cheryl drove him back to the picnic as if they hadn't made love. Doug just couldn't feel bad about making love to his daughter's best friend. Kids today, after all, had sex all the time. They watched too much MTV, that was the problem. If Cheryl happened to find boys her own age worthless, Doug had to say he agreed with her. Cheryl had only shown good sense in wanting to sleep with him.

Mayor Sweeney latched onto Doug as soon as he got back to the park, making Doug treasure the time with Cheryl all the more. By now, the hot dogs had all been eaten, and the senior citizens were tossing horseshoes. Between the drone of Sweeney nattering on about the perfect weather and how the whole nation would see the best face of Punderson and the clanging of each "ringer" at horseshoes, a brief moment opened up when both obnoxious sounds temporarily fell silent.

"Why's he so special? I'm just as ordinary as him, and nobody's ever made a fuss over me."

Doug stood still and furiously turned his head. All he could see were the geezers wrapped up in the horseshoe game or kids stuffing their faces with ice cream.

The words burned his ears. If he found that person who dared whisper them, he'd give him a piece of his mind. This day wasn't because he was ordinary. It was because he was extraordinarily ordinary. He was ordinary in a way that made him a mirror of everything decent in this country. He, Douglas Ford, was not a common man. He was the representative of the common man.

"I thought the parade went so well that we should do it again at 6:30," Sweeney said. "That way the networks can carry it live on their evening broadcasts."

Doug's first instinct was to say no, to let the idea die. Nobody wants to be out at 6:30, he thought. They would want to be at home with their TV sets and watch the recorded highlights of his parade.

But then the voice of the griper rang in his ears. Why not have a second parade, he thought. That would show that bastard how everyone really loved Doug Ford. The griper would have to shut up then. Maybe he'd even come to Doug after the second parade and apologize. "I was wrong, Mr. Ford. You really are wonderful."

"A second parade is a great idea," Doug said.

The limo took him home. As he rode, Doug thought of Barbara. Making love to Cheryl had really been an eye opener. His wife was old. She had let herself go. She really needed one of those tuck jobs or whatever to make herself attractive again. All of that loose skin had to go.

He glanced out the window and noticed something odd. They were driving past a house that didn't have his picture up anymore. He was sure the house had had the picture from the <u>Tribune</u> in the window when he passed this way on his way to the park. Why had they taken it down already?

Doug frowned and leaned back in his seat. Punderson needed a second parade. They needed to be reminded of how special he really was.

When he walked through the door, Barbara gave him a big hug. He could smell that she had cooked ribs and potatoes, his favorite meal. Doug got annoyed. She would probably want him to stay home and eat it.

"There's going to be a second parade, at 6:30. I won't have time to eat that meal."

Her face crumbled.

"It smells great, though," he said.

Barbara blinked.

"Kim's gone over to Cheryl's. I thought we could have a romantic evening tonight."

"After the parade," Doug said. "Right now I need a sandwich."

On the limo ride back to the park, Doug noticed with irritation that five houses no longer displayed his picture.

Bastards, he thought. This parade would show them. Those pictures would go right back up and stay there until midnight.

At Arrowhead Park, Doug saw that only half as many people had gathered for this parade as compared to the first one. Even the band seemed smaller. He looked intently at the woodwinds, searching for Cheryl. She didn't seem to be there.

Mayor Sweeney started talking at 6:30 sharp. For the first time in the mayor's life, it seemed to Doug, words didn't come easily to the blowhard. Sweeney started to repeat his earlier speech, caught himself using the same words, and tried to change them creating awkwardly long pauses as he thought.

Doug began to tap his foot as he listened. The Mayor sounded like a kidnap victim in a gangster movie who has to keep up a string of happy chatter with a gun pointed at the back of his head. If people had to listen to Sweeney hem-and-haw long enough, Doug feared, they'd start to doubt Doug's many virtues.

Finally, mercifully, Sweeney stopped talking and gestured for Doug to come forward. Doug practically ran over and grabbed the mike. He looked at the crowd and felt only disappointment as he compared it to what had happened hours before.

"I'd like to thank you all for coming here this evening," he said.

"You're welcome, tubby!" someone shouted.

A snicker ran through the crowd.

"Hey!" Doug saw red. "This is my day. You wouldn't want me to mouth off on your day, if you ever had a day. Show me respect. The networks came here today because of me. I put you on the map. You don't want Punderson to look like a town of ungrateful jerks, do you?"

The crowd stared in sullen silence. Doug turned away from them, and Mr. Caprillorio struck up the band while Doug got in the convertible.

It was a different march from this afternoon. People started to sing along.

"What's the matter with Doug Ford? He's okay.

What's the matter with Doug Ford? He's okay."

Doug's mouth hung open. The tune sounded lazy and flat, and the singing just felt lethargic, as if nobody really cared about him.

As the convertible drove around Punderson, nobody came out to cheer him either. He could see TVs on in different homes, and shrugged. They were probably watching this afternoon's parade, the better one, on TV.

The convertible turned a corner, and Doug could see someone pulling the Trib's Douglas Ford poster out of his window and balling it up like it was scrap paper.

He could see in the picture window of the next house perfectly. On the TV screen, Lucille Ball was working on an assembly line at a chocolate factory.

His face flushing, Doug looked back at the parade behind him. As people marched past their own homes or those of their friends, they dropped out of the parade.

I guess they never liked me, he thought. Not really.

The convertible turned down another street, and Doug saw Mr. Malkuczak, Kim's geometry teacher, standing there sprinkling his yard, utterly unconcerned by the parade.

"Hi, Mr. Malkuczak!" Doug waved at the man.

The teacher started and blinked at Doug. Then he smiled.

"Hey, Ford! Your daughter blows dogs!"

Chuckling and looking quite pleased with himself, the geometry teacher went back to sprinkling his lawn.

Doug's mouth hung open as he tried to cope with what he had heard. He looked back and saw the marching band stop playing because they were laughing so hard. A few even started to bark. In front of Doug, Mayor Sweeney shook with laughter.

"Shut up!" Doug leaned forward. "Kim's a sweet girl."

Sweeney just howled with glee.

Doug slapped the mayor in the ear with the back of his hand. The Mayor nearly slammed into the door.

"Stop this car!"

Rubbing his ear, Mayor Sweeney glared at Doug.

"Get out and walk, you son of a bitch. Walk home and fix your daughter up with Rin Tin Tin. Nobody treats me like this. No more garbage pickup for you, and tomorrow the property assessor will be around to fuck you in the ass. Now, get out of my car."

Not quite believing all this, Doug got out of the car. The paraders looked at him in smug silence, smiling, glad to see him brought low.

Doug looked around and estimated he was eight blocks from home. He'd get there and sit tight for the rest of the night, and this craziness would blow over.

He set off down Wellington, telling himself that Sweeney was a windbag, Malkuczak was weird, and that he should have left Punderson after college.

What a town. They couldn't stand to see anyone succeed, because that just reminded them of their own failure. What a bunch of jealous assholes, he thought.

A kid, maybe seven years old, rode toward him on a red bicycle. He looked normal at least, and Doug smiled at him.

The kid saw Doug and smiled. His bike squealed to stop in front of Doug.

"Mr. Ford, my Great Dane has a hard on for your daughter," the boy said.

Doug blinked and then slapped the kid's mouth. The kid fell off his bike and started to cry. Doug walked away from him.

Fuck the kid, Sweeney, Malkuczak, and all the lying sons of Punderson, he thought.

The sound of the kid crying followed him down the street, and it made Doug glad.

He could hear somebody talking to the kid and turned around. It was two band members. One pointed at Doug.

"Doug Ford tried to blow a little boy!"

Doug began to run. This had gotten too crazy. He had to get to his car and get out of Punderson tonight. Maybe everybody could have a good laugh about this tomorrow, but this night had gotten way out of control.

His chest pounded as his home came into view. His leg muscles burned as he ran up the driveway.

"Turned on you, did they?" Ann asked. She sat in a lawn chair under her carport and smoked a cigarette. "Not surprising, I suppose."

Doug threw open the side door of his house. The sound of TV wafted over him.

"Barbara, get in the car now! We've got to get out of here!"

Barbara didn't say anything for a moment.

"You're not on <u>Biography</u> tonight. They're running the life of Shemp Howard instead."

"Barbara!"

"It's really interesting," she said. "Did you know that he was the emotional anchor that kept the Three Stooges on an even keel?"

I have real problems, Doug thought, as a rock smashed through the front window.

The band had reached the house. They played the same march, but the words people sang were new.

"Everybody hates Doug Ford, he should burn."

Doug ran for his car. He got to the door when the first rock hit him. Two more soon followed, and he fell against the car. Two bandsmen caught him by the ankles and dragged him down the driveway as he pleaded for them to stop.

They stopped halfway down the driveway, and then the kicks started. They went for his gut, and then when they turned him over, they kicked him in the genitals and in the face.

"Stop! Stop!"

It was Ann. Doug sighed and remembered this morning, and how she had knelt on the bed for him. He opened his eyes and looked up at her.

"You dirty shit," she said and kicked him in the eye.

The crowd cheered. People stood on his hands while Doug tried to twist free.

Then he smelled gasoline and started to whimper.

A wave of laughter ran through the crowd as Mayor Sweeney and Mr. Caprillorio poured the liquid over Doug. He couldn't sit up but raised his arms as if beseeching them to stop.

Mrs. Wheeler lit a match and threw it at Doug. Cheryl did the same.

Douglas Ford howled as the flames ran across his body. The crowd cheered as the orange flames leaped into the twilight while his skin blackened and split. After a while, they began tossing their posters and photos of Doug onto the fire.

Some volunteers climbed the water tower and began to paint over Doug's face.

The day for Douglas Ford had ended.

Tomorrow would be someone else's day.

The Tale of the Three Pig Princes

Once upon a time, there lived three pig princes: Peter, Pippin, and Paul. They were the only children of Patrios V, King of Porkania.

When Patrios died, Peter, Pippin and Paul met with their mother, Queen Sooee, to settle on who would succeed to the throne, as primogeniture was rejected by pigs.

"We do not give our crown to the oldest son and let the other princes have nothing," Queen Sooee said. "That may be the custom of the wolves. We pigs are more civilized. Our king shall be the one of you who best shows how to deal with those lupine intruders."

She summoned Peter, Pippin and Paul over to a banquet table, upon which sat three covered dishes.

"Following the traditions of our kind," she said, each of you will select a place at the table. When I clap, please uncover your dish. He that has the straw shall take charge of Porkania and first face the problem of the wolves. If he succeeds, king he shall be. But if he fails, he that has the stick shall rule and face the problem of the wolves. The one who finds the brick shall be third."

Peter, Pippin and Paul took their places around the banquet table. When their mother clapped, they uncovered their dishes and discovered that Paul had found the straw, Pippin the stick, and Peter the brick.

Sooee, Peter and Pippin promptly knelt before Peter, who looked with unbelieving eyes at the straw he held.

"It's mine," he said. "I am to deal with the wolves."

He walked over to the window, regarded the land over which he now ruled, breathed deeply, and turned to his brothers.

"Send a messenger to Magnus Malefic Lupus and tell him that I wish to settle the differences between our two kinds once and for all. Let us draw up a treaty and have peace."

Pippin started as if slapped, but Peter's expression remained mask-like.

"Very well." Peter nodded to his brother. "I'll send my squire."

The squire departed and, most remarkably, returned intact to report that Magnus Malefic Lupus agreed with Prince Paul's request and would come to a treaty ceremony on the twelfth day of Henwen.

Relieved pigs pitched gaily-colored tents in the Great Field of Hogbeth, and laborers built a platform large enough to carry two thrones. The sun shone brilliantly on the appointed day as Magnus Malefic Lupus and forty wolves marched onto the Great Field at noon. An equal number of elegantly attired pigs awaited the wolf delegation. Prince Pippin and Prince Peter, however, had pointedly not been invited to the ceremony by their brother, who was weary of their criticism.

Each of the wolves wore a long scarlet robe that hung straight to the ground and swished elegantly as they marched across the grass. Never had the wolves seemed so large to the pigs. Never had the pigs seen the wolves so close. Their eyes were so big. Their teeth were so big.

Prince Paul stared at Magnus Malefic Lupus as if hypnotized. After a several seconds of embarrassing silence, he stirred himself and signaled for a fanfare of welcome to be played by the trumpeter pigs.

As the last notes died away, Prince Paul stood.

"With this treaty," he said, "we end the hostilities between our two kinds." He then recapitulated the sad and turbulent relations between the pigs and the wolves, going back to, if not the dawn of time, then much farther back than his listeners wanted to hear.

Magnus Malefic Lupus stood very still during this recitation of past misdeeds, but his eyes stayed busy counting every pig in the Great Field of Hogbeth. Finally, aware that Prince Paul had, blessedly, stopped speaking, Magnus Malefic Lupus strode forward and spoke.

"Fellow wolves. Dear pigs. The sad troubles between our two kinds need to be ended, not just by words, but by deeds."

He now reached under his cloak and pulled out a dirk, which he shoved into the throat of the startled Prince Paul.

His forty wolf retainers instantly drew their weapons and fell on the pigs nearest to them. Great was the slaughter in the field of Hogbeth that day. Blood splattered on the tents so proudly pitched for the occasion, and Magnus Malefic Lupus and his pack walked off with the trumpets that had blown a fanfare for peace.

Prince Pippin was bowling with his friends when the first survivor of the massacre reached him with the sad news.

"It's war!" He looked at his friends. "I knew no good could come of that foul treaty."

Pippin strode away from his unfinished game.

"Your highness," one of his friends said. "Should we abandon the game? You're winning."

"No time for that," Pippin said, with a toss of his head. "Warfare can't wait."

His friends spread this saying, and it soon became a watchword for the pigs, as any who could carry a spear rushed to Pippin's banner to avenge the field of Hogbeth. Within a week, Pippin had his host marching to the border of Wolvia.

An effigy of Prince Paul hung upside down from the grim sign that told all and sundry that here began the land of Wolvia.

"Strike that toy down and burn it," Pippin said. "But leave the sign. When we return, I shall hang Magnus Malefic Lupus himself on it."

The pigs cheered, banging their spears on their shields.

Prince Peter approached his brother.

"What lies beyond that ridge?" he asked.

Pippin shrugged.

"Wolvia," he said.

"Any rivers? Where are the wells for drinking water? Where is Magnus Malefic Lupus and how many wolves are with him?"

"You suggest that I leave the field of Hogbeth unavenged?"

"I suggest sending out scouts before blundering about with our army."

"Am I a blunderer?"

"You don't even know where your enemy is or what he can do to you."

Pippin glared at his brother.

"I am more concerned with what I shall do to him." He waved Prince Peter away, then pointed his spear at Wolvia.

"Forward!"

The pigs marched into Wolvia and found no wolves beyond the ridge. Nor did they see any later that day, or the next day, or the day after that. Every wolf lair that the pigs found lay empty. Every well they found had a dead lamb at the bottom of it. Thirst lashed the pig horde, and many became ill.

Finally, at noon on the fourth day of the invasion, as the pigs trudged onward, the foremost of the horde saw smoke billowing up ahead. Five wolves could be seen as they set a lair on fire.

A shout rose from every pig throat. These were the first wolves seen all campaign. It would be first blood for Hogbeth.

"Strike them down!" Pippin pointed his sword at the five.

The foremost pigs charged, but their stubby legs limited the ground they could cover. The five wolves loosed a flight of arrows and struck down two pigs. Then the wolves turned and loped away.

"Slaughter them as they have slaughtered us!" Pippin waved his sword as if he could kill all five. "No mercy."

The wolves now turned, loosed a second volley, then seemed to vanish into the brush.

"What trickery is this?" Peter asked, motioning for the pigs nearest him to stop.

By now the foremost pigs had reached the spot where the wolves had disappeared.

"A valley!" one of them called back.

"Get them!" Pippin waved his sword again, and the foremost pigs began to rush down the slope.

"Pippin! Wait!"

The Prince ignored his brother and rushed down the slope with the front ranks of the pig horde. They squealed with rage as they ran, while the five wolves kept well ahead of them, stopping occasionally to loose another flight of arrows.

As the first pigs reached the floor of the valley, a high-pitched yipping broke out. Arrows flew from the opposite side of the valley, as a wolf horde now rushed from the far end of the valley, toward the pig vanguard.

Peter had reached the lip of the valley and extended his arms, to prevent those pigs nearest him from rushing down into the trap.

"Form a square, Pippin! Form a square!" Peter shouted.

Even as his words left his lips, Peter could see that Pippin and the pigs around him had no chance. Startled, disorganized, struck by remorseless arrows, they found the climb back up the valley too exhausting. Seeing the bulk of his horde shot down around him, Pippin raised his spear and charged at the lamb-tailed standard of Magnus Malefic Lupus.

Pippin covered only a third of the distance to his target when a red-robed wolf felled him with a broadsword.

Peter turned away from the valley. He looked at the pigs who stood by him.

"Back to Porkania," he said.

"And abandon our brothers?" a young pig asked.

"If we stay here and fall, who will defend Porkania?" Anger burned behind Peter's words. "Retreat."

A score of wolves climbed from the valley and howled at Peter's band, but when they saw that he was truly retreating, they hurried back to the field of slaughter to loot the corpses of Pippin's band.

Peter marched his pigs for the rest of that day and the whole of that night, resting only in the morning after the battle, when it started to rain. Each time he rested his host, he made the pigs raise a palisade first.

"Get used to fighting behind walls," he said. "Magnus Malefic Lupus will be bringing the war to us soon enough."

Peter's pigs reached Porkania without serious losses. Peter then ordered the crops harvested or burned and the harvest to be stored in the capital, Snoutavia. He used some of the corn to bribe ten ravens to see what Magnus Malefic Lupus was doing.

The ravens brought back word that Magnus Malefic Lupus had summoned all wolves for an attack on Snoutavia and had built a catapult to knock down the walls of the pigs' city. Fortunately, the catapult itself delayed the wolves' progress, as its huge wheels often became mired in the muddy roads. Finally, after much cursing, Magnus Malefic Lupus ordered the infernal machine abandoned.

Peter gave the ravens more corn and pulled down the houses that stood outside the walls of Snoutavia. Extra water was drawn from the wells and stored in the attics of all buildings, in case the wolves used fire arrows.

Finally, on the 27th day of Fidum, Magnus Malefic Lupus raised his lamb-tailed standard on the Gondow Hill, a low rise outside Snoutavia. He sent his cousin, a young wolf in yellow boots, a crimson cape, and a white-plumed hat, to speak to the pigs.

"Dearest pigs," the young wolf said, and made a sweeping bow. "End this foolish war between us. Tear down your walls, give us those pigs who dare to call themselves royal, and accept Magnus Malefic Lupus as your master, and you shall live. See!" He pointed to a white banner next to the lamb-tail standard. "Surrender now, and all will live. When the red banner is raised, all who bear arms will be slain, but the sows and piglets shall be spared."

The young wolf smiled and shrugged. "When the black banner is raised, all pigs must die."

An arrow cut short his speech and his life. At a gesture from Magnus Malefic Lupus, the white banner fell and the red banner took its place. The wolves launched a volley of arrows, and two curious pigs fell from the walls.

"Keep low," Peter said. "Don't show yourselves. The Wolf has got to attack us. He'll do anything he can to get us out of the walls to attack him, so stay put."

For each day, the wolves taunted the pigs. Just outside bowshot, the wolves made a great show of drinking water, eating meat, and dancing on good meal they spilled on the ground.

Each day, Peter watched the wolves cavort and worried. He could see no siege engines among the tents of the wolves, nor did the ravens bring him word of any. Nor could he see any effort made to storm the walls of Snoutavia.

"Surely Magnus Malefic Lupus must have some other plan than simply luring us out of Snoutavia to our deaths," he said to himself.

He sent the ravens to count the wolves, and he counted all the wolves he could see. He tallied these numbers and found they could not hope to fill all the tents that the ravens saw pitched around Snoutavia.

Where were the missing wolves, Peter wondered. Part of the wolf horde must be elsewhere, but what target would tempt Magnus Malefic Lupus to send much of his army away from the main fight at Snoutavia. He could not think of one.

Turning from the wolf camp, Peter looked at the roofs of Snoutavia. He remembered how he had ordered water be stored in the attics of each building in case the wolves used fire arrows. So far they had not, and the hauling of water seemed like wasted effort.

So the enemy has not struck at us from above, Peter thought. But what if he should strike at us from below?

In an instant, Peter raced down from the wall toward the basement of the great keep of Snoutavia. He ordered the drummers to follow him.

"Bring me uncooked beans!" he ordered as he ran past a kitchen.

When he reached the basement of the keep, he had the drummers lay their drums on the ground on their sides. When the sow from the kitchen came, Peter directed her to put the uncooked beans on the skins of the drums.

Almost immediately, the beans began to dance, hopping about on the drumheads. The drummers stared, not believing their eyes, but Peter nodded grimly.

"The wolves are tunneling."

Magnus Malefic Lupus had not sent part of his horde away. He was having them tunnel under the walls of Snoutavia.

"Bring the water down from the attics," Peter said. "And start boiling it."

Peter ran up the stairs and ordered the stoutest pigs to come down to the basement of the great keep and begin to sink a counter-tunnel. Study swine with broad backs hurried to obey. A skeleton force remained on the walls to loose arrows at the wolves' camp, while Peter rallied the rest of his pigs to make a sortie out the front gate.

Finally, the pig counter-tunnelers ceased their work and hurried back to the surface, past steaming kettles of water. Below them, the muffled curses of the wolves could be heard as the predators hacked away at the dirt. Finally, wolf picks broke through into the pigs' counter-tunnel.

"What in furry blazes is this?" the first wolf shouted in the moment before a cauldron of boiling water poured down upon his head.

Cauldron after cauldron of hellishly hot water dumped down upon the baffled wolves, while the pigs waved their hats from a window as a signal to Peter.

"Open the gate!"

At Peter's command, the gates of Snoutavia wrenched open, and the pig host charged out at the startled wolves. The bulk of the wolf horde had lined up to go into the tunnel and now stood baffled by the screams of their comrades beneath the earth and the alarms of those guarding the camp.

"The pigs are charging! The pigs are upon us!"

Peter led the pig host into the wolf tents, slaughtering the guards that did not run away.

"Forget the tunnel! Save the camp!" Magnus Malefic Lupus shouted as he ran about, trying to turn his warriors to face the lines of the pig host.

"Javelins now!"

At Peter's command, a cloud of javelins rose into the air and fell upon the panicky wolves. Their nerves failed them, and they ran for their lives, all discipline forgotten, as sword-wielding pigs attacked and struck them down without mercy.

Seeing that the day was lost, Magnus Malefic Lupus ran as well. He put his camp far behind and ran until he reached a river. Here he stopped to take a drink, when three wolf archers came up behind him.

"You brought us to this ruin," they said.

They grabbed him, and as he begged for mercy, they strangled him with a bowstring. They were stripping his body of its golden breastplate and rings when five pigs ran up and quickly dispatched them. Seeing the gold, the pigs realized this was the body of Magnus Malefic Lupus, and they struck its head off and carried it back to Peter.

The pigs of Snoutavia burned the wolves abandoned tents, filled in both ends of the tunnel leaving the bodies of the wolves inside, and hung joyous purple banners from the walls of their city. A week after the end of the siege, on the first day of Sugsug, Queen Sooee herself placed the iron crown of Porkania on the brow of Peter II, King of the Pigs and the Vanquisher of the Wolves.

Jackie Gingerbread

One fine spring day, a housewife decided to make a gingerbread boy. She mixed up the batter, shaped it, and put it into the over. After setting the timer, she went into the living room to iron as she watched <u>All Mom's Children</u>.

Shortly before the timer should have gone off, the housewife thought she heard a thump from the kitchen. Standing the iron up, she walked over and saw that the gingerbread boy had jumped out of the oven and was starting to walk across the floor.

"Stop!" The housewife cried out. She bent over to catch him.

The gingerbread boy turned to her and gestured rudely with his little arms.

"Blow it out your batzinka, borkster!"

The gingerbread boy laughed to himself as he ran outside.

The housewife did not run after him, for she was doubled-over with laughter. Tears ran down her cheeks.

"Whoever heard of a garbaged-mouthed gingerbread boy?" she asked the air once she caught her breath.

By then the gingerbread boy had reached the driveway, where the husband was just pulling in. Getting out of his rusty Ford, the husband frowned at the gingerbread boy.

"Where do you think you're going?"

"Out of my way, zundo, or I'll double-knot your dangler!"

The husband exploded with laughter, and his beer-belly shook. His wife, still laughing, came to the back door.

"Isn't he a scream?" she asked. "And to think I was going to eat him."

"Go skervitzky yourself, borkster!"

The couple nearly fell over. Only the fact that he could lean against the Ford saved the husband from falling on his bottom.

"You… you should go to that comedy place," the husband said, as he wiped the tears from his eyes. "The Barnyard in the Courtyard. I'll get you the address."

The husband was as good as his word. He and the housewife wished the gingerbread boy good luck, and he set off to find the Barnyard in the Courtyard.

At the Barnyard, a bull sat in the office reading <u>Variety</u>. He looked up as the door opened, saw the gingerbread boy, and said:

"The kitchen's in the back. I book the acts, not the entrees."

"Why don't you sit on a toreador, Ferdinand? I'm not food for anybody."

The bull snorted with amusement. "You a comedian?"

"Did you take too many hits from the picador last time?" the gingerbread boy asked. "Of course I'm a comedian. I left a housewife and her husband streaming their knupfers, they were laughing so hard."

The bull thumped his desk with his hoof.

"Okay, you can warm up the crowd Friday night for Mickey Shemp. You got a name?"

"Gingerbread boy."

"That kind of name went out with the nickelodeon, kid." The bull frowned for a second. "Joey Gingerbread? Gingerbread Jack? Jackie Gingerbread?"

The spicy comedian snapped his fingers.

"Jackie Gingerbread." He nodded his head. "I'll be here Friday."

"Don't let 'em eat you alive," the bull said.

The Friday night crowd was a bunch of pigs, smelling of sweat and slop, looking for some laughs before the butcher called. They had all come to see Mickey Shemp do the blue material from the party album.

"Put your hooves on the radio," one fat porker squealed, quoting a line from Mickey Shemp's most famous routine.

Then the music started, the house lights went down, and a gingerbread boy walked into the spotlight. Disgruntled oinks filled the smoky air.

"Get back in the oven!"

"That's pretty brave talk for a future pork chop," Jackie Gingerbread said. He strutted across the stage. "What's wrong, pal? Not enough garbage in your slop today?"

The pig's friends laughed and smacked him with their hooves.

"That's right, that's right," Jackie Gingerbread said. He sneered. "He ain't no Easter ham. No pork chop can talk to me like he's top of the food chain."

Squeals of laughter shook the Barnyard in the Courtyard.

A half hour later, Jackie Gingerbread strutted backstage, the owner of the audience. Even the bull looked impressed.

"Kid, I thought they'd eat you alive. I'd have bet my krukas on it."

"Lucky you didn't, or you'd be a steer by now."

"I can make you a regular here."

Jackie could hear the pigs squealing for more.

"I'll take it."

Two weeks later, a couple of dogs sat at a far table, catching Jackie's act. They didn't laugh or applaud, but they did stick around for his second set. Jackie noticed them and their silence. It irked him, so instead of his usual second set, he started describing the "forbidden episodes" of <u>Brassie</u>, in which the star played hide the chawonga with Mrs. Dimple. Two pigs started hyperventilating and crashed to the floor, but the dogs just sat there and drank their toilet water. Jackie did think maybe he caught a glimpse of a smile once.

The dogs came back to his dressing room like they were joined at the hip. Herkle and Jerkle.

"No fire hydrants in here," Jackie said to them.

They shook their heads.

"This could be the biggest mistake of my life," the older dog finally said, "but we need to put together some commercials for no-stick cookware, and you're a natural for the concept."

"Just watch your mouth," the younger dog warned. "That <u>Brassie</u> stuff won't fly on TV."

"If I watched my mouth," Jackie said, "I'd have been eaten and sturbritched out by now."

Making the TV commercial proved the dullest work Jackie Gingerbread ever did. He had to lay down in a tray in a phony oven *forever*, while the director, a stupid horse who had started in the business directing second-unit on <u>Mr. Ed</u> and therefore considered himself a regular Erich Von Clydesdale, made sure that the lights were just right.

Meanwhile, the woman who had to open the over door had taken an acting lesson or two and motivated herself by going on about how much she liked her grandmother's cooking. For all that, she never opened the oven door the right way for Von Clydesdale, so Jackie could never pop out of the oven and say, with big brown eyes: "Don't eat me, but everything else you bake in Stick-Free Cookware will taste terrific!"

Finally, the oven door opened to Von Clydesdale's satisfaction and Miss Method pulled the damn tray out.

Okay, Jackie thought, now it's my turn to ruin a take.

He jumped out of the pan and snarled: "You can't cook this, razhooga!"

Von Clydesdale stamped his hooves so hard they put a hole in the floor. He cancelled the rest of the day's shooting and swore he'd never work with Jackie again, which was just fine with Jackie.

They cut Jackie's last word from the tape and ended on a freeze frame of his snarling face and brought in a voice man to coo:

"Maybe not this time, Mrs. Housewife, but anything else you bake in Stick-Free Cookware will taste terrific!"

Within two weeks "You can't cook this!" saturated the nation. T-shirts with Jackie's face and the saying sold like pet rocks did last Christmas. The actor who played the lazy son-in-law on Mac and the Moose took to growling the line once a show. Erich Von Clydesdale won a Cleo for the commercial, and Stick-Free sent Jackie two sets of pots and pans.

He tossed them in the trash.

He didn't need cookware. He had gotten something better out of that commercial: an invitation to Nightowl.

Everybody in the business knew that Oliver J. Barndoor could make a career or break it with a smile. All of the biggies had done well on Nightowl. Bruno and Buster had first done "The Two Thousand Year-Old Bear" on the show, and Polly Pinfeathers had introduced "Captain Kidd's Parrot" there to Barndoor's great delight. On the other side of the ledger, years before Jackie's time,

Rinty Rover had barked of his need to water a tree when he was Barndoor's guest. The smile on the owl's face froze, and Rinty had never been near network TV since. It was rumored he still did standup, but only in places where the clientele ate from the left side of the doggie dish.

Oscar J. Barndoor had great power and no regrets about using it. The smart money in the trade, the old zookums who knew Brassie when Brassie was a she, bet that Jackie would flop.

Jackie knew that was the way the smart money was laying. He wanted it that way.

Magic time.

"Oscar, big guy, how ya doin?" Jackie asked as he strode across the Nightowl stage like he owned the gizzhole.

As the owl extended a wing of welcome, Jackie turned to the audience and said:

"I'd let this guy cook me any time."

Oscar J. flashed a big smile, and the crowd roared its approval.

"You could cook me any time, Oscar," Jackie said. "But I wouldn't let that Mr. Frapple lay a finger on me."

The audience whooped in joy at the reference to the hyper-anxious TV character who had sold miles of toilet paper over the years.

"I was so afraid that he'd be the one opening that oven door," Jackie said. He shuddered. "I don't want him squeezing my Softies."

Oscar J. Barndoor hooted with glee.

"And I can't tell you how glad I was that I didn't have to break into commercials with the Flush-Away Man. I hear his dinghy's pretty dingy these days."

While Oscar J. laughed his approval, Jackie Gingerbread worked through a list of commercial characters that the audience was clearly tired of seeing. Oscar J. then let Jackie sit on the couch while the next act came up.

It was a hippie singer who had hit it big with a record that used a tune from J. S. Bach. Oscar J. tried to be nice to her, but Jackie couldn't stand her. When she said something about the war, it was too much for him.

"Why don't you move to Hanoi?" he asked. "You make me sick. I don't care if Bach writes your music, you don't deserve to live in this country!"

The audience gave him a standing ovation, and Oscar J. Barndoor smiled warmly.

Network executives called him the next day. They were impressed, *impressed*, by his rapport with the audience. He had touched a nerve. The country was ready for someone to say the things he was saying. They also had the perfect vehicle for his talents, a show in the tradition of <u>All in the Bunker</u>, but with whimsy. Think of it as a cross between <u>All in the Bunker</u> and <u>Hokey Bear</u>, and Jackie was the only performer who could make it work.

Was he interested?

Jackie gripped the phone and thought. His mouth had gotten him far. If he hadn't spoken up that first time, he would be a flushed away gavoot. He had out-talked a housewife, her husband, a bull, some pigs, a self-important horse, and a very important owl.

Could he out-talk a nation?

No problem.

Great, great, great, the executives gushed. He could sign the papers with Mr. Reynaud tomorrow at lunch.

Jackie strolled into the network dining suite and sensed trouble. Mr. Reynaud sat in an overstuffed chair and fiddled with a hearing aid. His foxy face looked annoyed.

"Who are you?" he asked.

"Jackie Gingerbread, the new star comedian."

The old fox swung a paw dismissively.

"There's always a new star comedian. Every week there's a new one."

"What comedian do you like?" Jackie asked.

"Ned Skeleton." Mr. Reynaud raised a paw. "He has real talent."

A sneer crossed Jackie's face. What an embarrassment Skeleton was. That guy had more dead fans than living ones.

"If he's a skeleton, he should be buried," Jackie said.

Mr. Reynaud looked at the gingerbread boy and shut off his hearing aid.

"I'm a little deaf," he said. "Come over here and say that again."

Jackie took three steps. "I said if he's a skeleton, they should bury him."

The fox's eyes twinkled in a kind, grandfatherly way.

"Closer please. I really want to hear what you're trying to say.

Jackie sighed, took five steps, and yelled as loud as he could.

"I said, redbutt, that if he's a skeleton, he should be buried!"

Mr. Reynaud pointed at his ears.

"It's hell getting old, kid. Just come a little bit closer, and I'll hear you just fine."

Sighing, Jackie walked up to the end of the fox's snout.

"You dumb schlupflehead, I said…"

And Mr. Reynaud's jaws closed on Jackie Gingerbread's head.

Later, as he told the story to his fellow network executives, Mr. Reynaud admitted that while the gingerbread had been too bitter to taste good, he could not remember the last time he had enjoyed the act of eating so much.

After You Come Others

A hot-air balloon, red-and-green stripes above a roaring orange flame, rose into the twilight sky. I blinked through my windshield. This was the absolute last thing I expected to see on the east side of Taylorville.

"Where's Fellini?" I asked and started looking for a place to park.

The evening might turn out to be a good one after all, I hoped, turning off from Rutherford into the park. I had intended to see Mean Streets and Taxi Driver at the New Carnegie, only to find that they'd had their power shut off. Instead of driving back the way I came, I decided to cut west to the freeway.

The drive had been like passing a touring company production of Taxi Driver, sleazy and threatening, but not as powerful as the original.

"All the animals come out at night," I said, quoting De Niro.

When Rutherford began to ascend into some hills, the area improved. The futuristic glass and steel structures of the Taylorville Clinic rose to the right of the street. The park and festival were to the left. As I pulled into the park, I noticed the large, reddish Bronson Memorial atop a hill. I had to be on the backside of Lakeland Cemetery, I decided.

People had parked on the grass by the rapid transit line, so I did the same, then walked to the admission table. I gave five bucks to a gray-haired woman wearing a T-shirt of a threatening wizard, and she stamped a purple dot on the back of my right hand.

The hot air balloon roared again as I entered the festival grounds. A lot of the booths were arts and crafts, imitation Medieval next to authentic East Central Europe. I stopped by the puppet theater for a bit. The skit spoofed Wagner's Ring, with the Siegfried puppet complaining about how smelly dragon blood was. The kids laughed.

"She's supposed to be here tonight."

I turned to look at the speaker of that line, a short, stocky nervous blond man. He sported snake tattoos on both arms, from elbow to wrist. I had never seen an uglier face. It gave the impression that his nose and mouth were too small. He talked to two friends, all three wearing black T-shirts and blue jeans. Their faces resembled his, with small noses and mouths.

I looked at some of the other people, to compare faces, when I turned back to the trio, they were gone.

As Siegfried burned his feet getting to Brunhilde, I walked off toward the balloon. A ride in that would make the evening worthwhile.

The balloon cost $5 extra. No wonder the line was short. Still, I didn't ride in a balloon every day, so I got in line.

Immediately, a one-armed man was behind me. I turned and thought he was Santa Claus, all jolly eyes above a white beard. His cap killed that idea. It looked like the kind of thing WWII partisans wore, only with the insignia cut away.

"Interesting cap," I said.

"Does it bother you?"

"No. I'm not in the INS."

One of the three ugly guys came by, looking at the people in the balloon line. The one-armed man turned away from him, rather obviously I thought, but the ugly guy didn't notice and walked on.

"He wasn't looking for you," I told the old man. "He's looking for some woman. I heard him say that to his friends."

"You did?"

"There are three of them, looking for 'she.'" I said.

"It's time for our ride," he said.

The old man and I got into the basket with the pilot. The roar over my head during the ascent drove me mad, but when we reached the end of the tether and had quiet, I loved seeing Taylorville in the twilight, its skyscrapers and streetlights sparkling in the gathering dusk. The lake brooded to the north, and the Bronson Memorial loomed like the Gothic Revival pile it was meant to be.

Taylorville as fantasyland? I snorted.

The balloon descended slowly, and I helped the old man out of the basket.

"You should have your fortune told," he said to me as we walked away.

"I don't believe in that stuff."

He shrugged. "You don't have to believe. It would just be a part of all this." He gestured with his hand, taking in the booths, the puppet show, the crowd.

"I can see that," I said. "I just don't want to spend a lot of money on it."

"No, no. See that striped tent over there?"

It was a small green-and-white tent, with a sign resting against the front that said FORTUNES.

"Just tell her that Milovan sent you, and you won't have to pay."

"Oh."

"It won't cost you anything."

Now I felt I had to go or else Milovan would be offended.

"Thanks," I said.

"Take care."

Walking over to the fortune teller, I saw another of those ugly guys. He nearly walked into me, as he looking inside the tents instead of watching where he was going.

"Hey, I'm standing here," I said.

He looked at me and growled. It was a real growl, like a dog's. Then he stepped aside and hurried on.

I stepped into the FORTUNES tent. The odor of strong tobacco assaulted me. My eyes got used to the candlelit murk, and I sat down at the table in front of an old, dark woman. She put her pipe aside and looked at me warily.

"Milovan sent me," I said. "I want my fortune told."

The mention of the name made her eyes light with interest. She regarded me carefully, as if judging me somehow.

"Show me your right palm."

I held it out. She looked at it, nodded, and signaled for me to go.

"After you come others," she said.

Well, it was free, I thought, but what kind of fortune was that?

You will take a dangerous journey. You will meet a beautiful woman. *Those* were fortunes. But "after you come others"? That could describe standing in line for license plates.

As I stepped out of her tent, I saw the setting sun directly behind the Bronson Memorial, making the building look like the product of Bram Stoker's imagination. Maybe I could walk over and see it up close before all the sunlight was gone.

Some people had started to strike their tents. A tall woman in a blue jean dress was taking down paintings and putting them in her van. I walked over to look at the three still on display.

They went together, all dealing with brooding mountainscapes and dark figures lurking around the edges. Looking at them in the shadow of the Bronson made me uneasy.

"What do you think?" she asked.

I looked at her and knew I was doomed. Her face was too wide for conventional beauty, but her prominent cheekbones and strong eyebrows made her very exotic.

"You have a lot of talent," I said.

"It's only a hobby," she said, taking down one of the paintings and carrying it to her van. "It makes me happy."

Happy? I looked at the second painting, of dark shapes gathering around a tree on a mountaintop. Not the first word I would have chosen.

"Hey, Shura, how ya doin?"

I turned and saw the leader of the three ugly guys, the one who had been so desperate to find some woman this evening. His face looked especially weird not.

"Fine," Shura said. "How are you and your friends?"

"They didn't come." He shrugged. "I'm here by myself tonight. You need help closing down, your highness?"
Shura put her hand in a big pocket on the front of her dress. "No thanks. I can close by myself."

"I'll help, if you'll let me," I said.

The guy grunted. "This is so far over your head, asshole. Just get out."

"He has two friends at the festival, Shura," I said.

Shura took a dagger out of her pocket. Its thick blade could do real damage.

"Where are they, Lar?" She walked up to him.

He glanced at me.

"Fucker," he said.

Shura stabbed him in the belly and pulled the blade upward. Lar slapped his hands over the wound and ran away. Blood covered Shura's blade, yet Lar ran as if he had only ripped a hangnail.

"Are you good with a dagger or sword?" Shura asked me.

"No," I said. "It hasn't come up before tonight."

She nodded, as if expecting that kind of answer and picked up her jean jacket. She drew a dagger from an inside pocket and gave it to me.

"Just get in close and do damage. Go for the throat if you get the chance. Lar and his pals are pretty vain, so it's good to go for their eyes too."

"Lar will be back?"

"He's a messenger. They don't have any sense."

Her nose twitched as she tried to sense danger. She didn't look entirely human anymore. Her nose and mouth had pulled forward, and her eyes seemed wider. For a moment I wanted to run, until I remembered Lar and his pals. I decided I had a better chance of survival with Shura.

If I ran now, she might use her dagger on me.

Shura threw the last of her paintings in the van and locked it. She started to walk toward the trees.

"I need to go this way," she said.

I followed, splashing across a creek into the trees. I hate wearing wet sneakers.

As we ran, I heard something splashing behind us. I looked back at Lar and his two ugly friends.

"After you come others," the fortune teller had said. That was accuracy I could have done without.

Shura and I ran up the hillside to a wrought iron fence. I assumed it was for Lakeland Cemetery, although I didn't see how they could get away with keeping the spikes on the top of the fence so sharp. That was a lawsuit waiting to happen.

Shura scrabbled up the fence and leaped down to the other side. I heard footsteps running through the trees. I began climbing.

I just got to the top, when one of them grabbed the fence. I jumped down inside the cemetery, as my pursuer started climbing. I turned, reached through the bars, and grabbed his foot with one hand. I brought my dagger forward and cut his Achilles' tendon.

He roared. His face looked like an enraged boar's. Shura ran up and cut his other tendon. He pulled at the bars with all his might. I thrust my blade up into his guts, and he roared.

Shura tapped my shoulder. "Come" she said, as the other messengers showed up. We ran back into the shadows of the cemetery, Shura looking more and more beastlike with each step. I paused, then heard the tread of our pursuers crunching on the gravel road. I ran after Shura. She might be frightening, but she liked me better than the guys back there did.

We took refuge behind a monument. I assumed it was a Civil War monument but then realized that the mounted general was pointing not with a sword but with his claws.

While I dealt with that, I realized that Shura smelled. Not the locker room stink of somebody who'd been fleeing from enemies. That was me. Her stink reminded me of the tiger enclosure at the zoo on a hot day.

I decided not to look at her face. I would look at her shoulder, which was safely covered by her jean jacket. That way I wouldn't run screaming into the night.

She poked me in the ribs and pointed. Lar and his buddy walked along a row of tombstones to our left. Shura shook with excitement. I shook.

Don't go for the chest, I thought. Go for a crippling wound: leg, arm or eye. Decapitation would be good, but it probably went beyond my skill.

Just two hours ago, I remembered, my biggest problem was the lack of electricity at the New Carnegie.

Lar turned toward us, and Shura leaped forward. I froze for a moment, then ran after her.

Shura had knocked Lar down, but his pal had gotten his arms around her. I grabbed his curly hair and pulled his head back, bringing my knife around.

He howled, but he let Shura go. She finished off Lar, then she cut my guy's tendons.

"Let's go to the tower," Shura said. "We probably have some time before an assassin gets here."

The immediate crisis over, Shura looked more human. Granted, she had very fine hair growing between her eyebrows and her thick hairline, but she smiled at me, and I smiled back. I kept hold of the dagger, however.

"What's all this about?" I asked.

"Politics," she said and started to run for the tower.

I had visited the memorial of Taylorville's greatest steel baron in the Fifth Grade, but while this tower stood on the same site as the Bronson Memorial, it was quite different. Seven stone gargoyles loomed off the top of this tower, each turning its head to watch as Shura and I approached.

Shura pulled an iron key out of her jacket and opened the massive creaky door. Her action released a musty smell that made me cough as we headed up the stairs.

"The king has gotten tired of my mother," she said, pausing on a landing beneath a slit of a window that let in some moonlight. "He remarried and now wants to eliminate the issue of his first marriage." She raised her dagger. "I don't intend to be eliminated."

As Lar can well testify, I thought.

After two more flights of stairs, we reached the door to the roof. Walking out into the night, I immediately went to the edge and looked at the lights of Taylorville.

The hills were there, and so was the lake, but the skyscrapers and electric lights had vanished. I could see a vast metropolis, yes, but the biggest building, which I had never seen before, had seven domes, and nothing stood taller than three storeys. Rising from the lake was a statue of a horned creature blowing a conch.

Shura took a golden arrow out of her jacket and hurled it into the air, where it burst into flame and split into three separate missiles flying into the darkness. I had barely enough time to register my amazement, when I heard the flapping of large wings.

A black-winged man flew toward us, the moonlight showing the maggots on his pale face. He swung a scimitar.

"An assassin, right, Shura?"

"Yes." Her face was getting beastlike again.

"Do you have other arrows or anything that could drop him?"

"No. Just let him land between us, and we'll finish him off."

It's good that you have enough confidence for the two of us, I thought, positioning myself diametrically opposite Shura.

Maggot-face landed between us, reeking of ancient graves. He struck at Shura, and I rushed at him, causing his wings to snap at me, but pulling him away from Shura. He thrust at her, but I charged at his back and slashed at his wings so her turned away again.

Maggot-face backhanded a blow at me. I tripped trying to avoid it. He laughed and wheeled to Shura, only she thrust forward with a roar, driving her dagger into his chest. The impact forced him back, so he tripped over my legs and crashed into the stone floor. His skull shattered, creating a small, whiny tornado of dust that skittered around the floor, growing taller.

A deeper moaning now began in the skies overhead, and I looked up to see a funnel cloud taking shape.

"Run!" Shura yelled, and I followed her down the stairs, as fast as I could. The moaning from the sky and the whining from the roof grew louder and louder.

Down and down we ran, until we reached the door and rushed out into the night. Shura fell face first on the grass. I did the same. Behind us, the moan met the whine, and the tower exploded. Bits of brick and dust showered down around us.

Some guys meet nice happy princesses who sing like birds, I thought.

Shura stuck her claws into the dirt and pushed herself upright.

But what would a guy like me do with a princess like that, I asked myself.

Shura now ran down the hill, deeper into the cemetery. As I started after her, the ground began to shake. The smell of brimstone filled the air.

"Hurry up!" Shura waved at me. "Arm yourself."

A number of helmets, breastplates and discarded weapons lay at the bottom of the hill. A cave sat nearby. The sort of cave, I thought, in which a dragon would live.

"Father's very desperate. He's waking the dragon," Shura said, picking up a helmet and a two-handed sword.

I grabbed a helmet off the ground and slapped it over my head. The only swords I could see were broken, but I spotted an iron pike. I picked it up, surprised by its weight.

The dragon roared and began pulling itself out of the cave, its dull, yellowed eyes fixed on Shura. I crouched and waited for it to get closer.

Shura flourished her sword as the beast leaped forward. I charged at the scaly green foreleg and fell to the ground as my pike clanked off the scale like a stick off the side of a tank.

Shura ran in beneath the dragon's head and struck at its pale white neck. Her blade drew blood, making the beast leap back. This dragon clearly leaped like a frog, and the white scales weren't as hard as the green ones.

The dragon looked at Shura and began to leap.

"Stay put!" I yelled, running in front of Shura, jamming the putt of my pike into the ground. I got the point aimed up just as the dragon's white belly came down.

The dragon bellowed, Shura roared, and I realized that Siegfried had been right. Being bathed in dragon's blood was hot, sticky, and unpleasant.

I wiggled out from under the dragon, while Shura struck its head off.

I just wanted a shower.

Three golden flames shot through the night sky, joined, and fell to Shura's feet as a golden arrow.

"Shura!" a voice called from the west.

I looked as a tall, dark-haired warrior with a two-bladed axe across his shoulders strode up to Shura.

"Udo," she said and kissed him.

I hoped it was a brother-sister kiss, but after a while, I decided it wasn't.

"Shura," another voice called from the east.

I turned to see a bury, red-bearded guy with two swords in his belt run forward to lift Shura in the air, turn her around and kiss her.

"Rothgar," she said.

"Shura," a third voice called from the south. Tall, blond, with an elegant mustache, this guy, I could see, had a longbow slung over his shoulder.

"Laymond," Shura said, running over to grip him fiercely and kiss him with passion.

A cloud passed over the moon, and it started to rain. The first drops hit the dragon blood on my cheek and washed it off. I had just noticed that it wasn't raining on Shura and her friends but only on me, when the deluge started.

Rain bucketed down. The dragon blood ran off me like it had never been there in the first place. I could hear the familiar click-click of the Green Line Rapid as it came out of the tunnel behind me.

The skies cleared, and Shura and her companions had vanished. I sprinted through the puddles and came to the cemetery fence, with its rounded tops. There were no sharp iron spikes anymore. If there ever had been.

"After you come others," I said to myself, as I remembered Udo, Rothgar and Laymond.

Boy, had I misread that fortune.

The festival had packed up and departed. My car was the only one left in the lot. As I ran over to it, I saw that some joker had slipped something over the antenna.

It was some kind of chain, and I grabbed it before letting myself into the car. I turned on the interior light and saw that it was a medallion. I looked at the inscription.

A tigerish woman's face, surrounded by the words KROLA SHURA III, looked up at me.

"Long may she reign," I said and kissed the image.

Ol' Stoneface Speaks

Thanks for finding a tape recorder with such wide buttons, Sam. That was thoughtful. So I'll just read your questions and answer them.

How has becoming a superhero changed my life?

That's a hard question. I mean, I don't really think of myself as a superhero. I know that I'm in the comic books, and they sell pretty well, but I don't consider myself a superhero.

Before, I always used to think of superheroes as being like Captain Courageous. He had a good job working for that TV station and from time to time had to step into a phone booth to take off his pants and save the world.

Okay, that sounds too bitter. I've met CC a few times, and he's a great guy. It's just that it's different when you can put on a costume to fight the bad guys, because when they're finished and you've beaten them, you just take the costume off and blend in with everybody else. When I was a kid, that's what I always thought of when I thought of superheroes: a guy with a neat costume.

That covers Captain Courageous, Amazonia, Kozmik Kid, Night Avenger....

But then there's me.

Let's face it, when Night Avenger puts the Maniac away for the ten thousandth time, he can take off those gray pajamas and go back to the mansion, pick up the phone, and invite any one of his girlfriends over to help him unwind. (Kids, don't let Mom know, but Susie Shannon is just a composite character to stand in for I don't know how many women who get excited...)

Okay, you'll have to cut that, I know. Sorry, Sam, I won't do that again.

I shouldn't have said it. Aaron is a decent guy. He's been at this far longer than I'll ever be, but he's still willing to teach a newcomer some pointers.

Like I was saying, at the end of the day, Aaron can take off his Night Avenger suit. Me, I've got gray rocks growing out of my skin. They don't come off.

Maybe it's good that they don't come off. If they came off, and the Gargoyle found out, he'd be here in a flash to pound me into bite-sized hamburger patties. Maybe too, if the rocks came off, and my face got in the paper, the U. S. government might look me up and give me the bill for all the hardware I turned into scrap metal when I first became Stoneface.

So maybe it's all for the best that I've got gray rocks growing out of my skin.

Maybe this is good in some other ways too. I mean, now I know why I never get any dates. Who the hell would want to go out with a big gray monster? I mean, beautiful women might pose with me and give me a bouquet for smashing all those Martian spaceships, but it never goes beyond handing me some stupid flowers.

Hell, before I was Stoneface, no woman would have been caught dead handing me a bouquet in the first place.

I never quite figured out why that was. It wasn't because I was ugly or anything. I knew I wasn't TV handsome, but I had the right number of eyes and ears, and my nose pointed the right way. I had to wear glasses, which I know some girls don't like, so I figured I'd get fewer dates than the guys who didn't wear glasses. But I never figured that I'd never go out at all.

I always hoped that after I talked to some girl for a while she would say: "Frank, I think it would be fun to go to the movies Friday night with you."

But that didn't happen.

The girls seemed to know that I wanted to ask them, and it was remarkable to see how they dealt with it. When I approached, they banded together in groups of three and four and talked about the lyrics on the latest albums or the grades on the chemistry labs. They left me no way I could separate out the one I wanted to ask out. Not once. They were like a caribou herd in those Wild Kingdom episodes Mr. Horton showed in Biology, and I was the Kodiak bear.

Sometimes, I might see two girls alone, and as I'd walk over, thinking the odds were now slightly in my favor, the one I wanted to ask out would suddenly say to the other one: "So Mom and I are going to have a girls' night out and go to the mall." And there I was, effectively pre-empted as Mr. Remarkable would say.

So I spent a lot of evenings at home alone reading comic books and watching sci-fi shows on TV. Now that I look back on it, it was almost like I was unconsciously giving myself training for my future life.

Sometimes I wonder what life would have been like if it hadn't been for that field trip. If I had never become Stoneface. Would I have dated Sonia Richardson?

When I wake up in the morning, and I'm lying there with the dawn slipping in through the blinds, and I'm not entirely sure I'm awake, and I almost think I'm still Frank Melnik, I can convince myself that had my senior year happened without that trip to Ziprontek Laboratories, I could have worked things out with Sonia.

But when I'm awake and sitting next to Johnny Blast while he makes bad puns as we jet halfway across the world to trade punches with the Screaming Six, I tell myself that I never really had a chance with her.

I don't know why I was so sold on her. She never really treated me different than the other girls did. The one time I got close to talk to her, she looked at my feet and said: "You have really big feet. What size shoe do you wear? Those are huge feet."

Remember, she said that *before* I became Stoneface.

I guess I liked her because she wasn't entirely accepted by the other girls. Her mom had been a DP, and most of the other kids held that against Sonia. And I thought that that was my opening. I was an outcast, and she was an outcast.

Only I guess I was an outcast with huge feet.

But I had managed to talk to her that time. And I told myself that things would go better the next time, and maybe even better the time after that, and that by the time graduation rolled around, I might have talked her into a date of some kind.

And then my Chem class went to Ziprontek Laboratories.

The funny thing is that I wasn't really excited about the "great" field trip that Miss Hoffman wrangled that spring. I knew nobody would want to sit next to me on the bus, Carl and Eddie would goof off and get us all in trouble, and I would face a mountain of homework from all the classes I missed when I got back. But everybody else in Chem oohed and ahhed over the chance to go to Ziprontek, like they were going to be offered a job there or something.

The only one who might get a job there was Sonia, who had already completed Chem II as a junior and was helping Miss Hoffman with my Chem class on her study hour, which was why she was coming on the field trip with us.

I didn't even hope she'd sit by me on the bus. I knew she would sit with Miss Hoffman, who would be talking to Sonia about the great future ahead of her in chemistry.

And that was the way the trip went. Nobody sat next to me on the bus. Miss Hoffman gave all her attention to Sonia, which Carl and Eddie took as a signal to have a fart contest, and when Miss Hoffman noticed that, she got really mad at all the boys on the trip.

We hadn't even gotten to Ziprontek, and I was feeling pretty blue, and I didn't even know that I had less than an hour to live as a normal human being.

The Carl and Eddie show continued once we got off the bus, Carl whispering dirty lyrics to every TV theme song he could think of, while Eddie started lying about how much booze he would put away this Friday night. Miss Hoffman, of course, was too busy introducing Sonia to Ziprontek employees and making sure the girls stood in front of the exhibits to really pay attention to this.

I just wanted to take two stones and smack Carl and Eddie over the head.

That was when the Matter-Transformer went haywire.

As everyone who has read Stunning Stories # 45 and Stoneface # 1 knows, Ziprontek was really a front for Count Zorndorf's latest scheme to destroy America. Unfortunately, the day of my field trip was the first time they tested the Matter-Transformer. I guess Zorndorf wanted everything in his evil plan to be ready to go by the anniversary of V-E Day, but there were just too many bugs in the system.

Personally, I like the Wolfe & O'Brien Stoneface # 1 version of my origin best. I know a lot of people like the Wolfe & Benko Stunning Stories version better because it's "edgier" while O'Brien draws me as "too heroic." Well, if a guy can't get to be heroic in his own origin story, I ask you, what's the point of living?

Anyway, I like that second version better because it isn't too accurate. Wolfe took the facts and made a good story out of them, telling how I stepped into that Matter-Transformer beam to save my girlfriend "Peggy."

Well, there was no "Peggy." I suppose Wolfe based her on Sonia, but I didn't step into any beam on purpose. The wall just blew out, and this purple light surrounded me as I was thinking my thoughts about smashing Carl and Eddie with stones, and suddenly my body starts this rippling that I'll never be able to describe. All I can say is that it felt good, the purple light, and I wanted more of it, and I was screaming with joy as my flesh bulked out and took on the characteristics of stone.

When I finished changing, I looked down on Carl and Eddie, saw their wet trousers and shameless terror in their faces, and knew that all my life had been a prologue to this moment.

That's when the rodent-men attacked them.

What if they hadn't? I ask myself that sometimes. What if the Matter-Transformer had turned those Ziprontek employees into slow-moving turtle-men or rooted-to-the-floor geranium-men? What if I had brought my stone fists down on Carl and Eddie and smashed them into goo before the horrified stares of my classmates? I wouldn't be Johnny Blast's traveling buddy then. I'd probably be part of the Screaming Seven.

But the rodent-men rushed in. They charged at Carl and Eddie, and for a second it looked like they would be the ones to dispatch my obnoxious classmates instead of me, the guy who had suffered with them all year.

I had listened to their stupid jokes, smelled their fats and put up with their insults. No stupid rodent-man had the right to kill *my* jerks.

So I pulled the rodent-men off Carl and Eddie, and I slammed my hands together. Carl and Eddie tore off down the hallway, and I've never seen them again. Now that I think about it, life without those two jerks was probably the first sign I had that life as Stoneface would be a good thing. At the time, however, no sooner had they run away when the Ziprontek security guards showed up to start blasting at me, and I had other problems.

Like I said earlier, all those comic books I had read and sci-fi that I'd watched came back to me as I tossed those security guys around like rag dolls and punched my way out of Ziprontek and ran screaming down the train tracks to the lake.

I never saw Miss Hoffman again or went back to Chester A. Arthur High School and that mountain of homework waiting for me. I never went back home either. I was living my own comic book now, and I didn't need my old collection any more.

Although sometimes I remember that I had the first ten issues of <u>Savage Sword of Grondar</u> in near mint condition, and I could kick myself for walking away from that when I hear how much they sell for now.

There was just one person I tried to see again after that day at Ziprontek. Sonia Richardson. It took me a while, because I was pretty crazy just after my transformation. Mr. Remarkable eventually located me (<u>Stunning Stories</u> # 48) and calmed me down and got me into Team Remarkable (<u>Stunning</u> # 49 and <u>Stoneface</u> # 2). I proved myself fighting Ghost Parasite and Vukovak (<u>Team Remarkable</u> # 75 and # 79 and <u>Stoneface Annual</u> # 1). The public began accepting Stoneface as a good guy, and I thought I could now see Sonia and let her know that beneath those gray rocks I was okay.

Mr. Remarkable didn't think that this was such a great idea, and he told me that I should let go of Frank Melnik and just think of myself as Stoneface. But he also knew he could say that to me again and again, and I could hear it over and over, but it wouldn't really take until I had lived it, so he said he'd try to arrange a meeting.

I think that everybody who reads <u>Team Remarkable</u> knows this on some level, but, really, Mr. Remarkable is the father I never had. It's a shame I could only meet him after I was no longer human but this gray rock monster, but I guess life is like that.

Anyway, he brought Sonia out to the Remarkable Building, supposedly to ask her about that day at Ziprontek, because any little detail she might still remember might help Team Remarkable in the search for Count Zorndorf, blah-blah-blah.

How could she not agree? And so she walked into my life again: poised, her strawberry blonde hair cut elegantly short like Dorothy Hamill's, her light blue eyes bright with enthusiasm at talking to the best-known scientist in America. When I saw her walk into the main conference room of the Remarkable Building, I remembered why I had always been attracted to her.

If only my memories of her ended at that moment.

She walked in, and I stood up and ran over to her, to take her hand in mine and say "Sonia, I'm okay, and it's great to see you."

But I was a gray, rock-covered monster running toward her, and those light blue eyes filled with terror as I thudded my way across the floor.

"Sonia! It's just me, Frank!" I yelled at her.

Maybe a voice forced out of a petrified mouth sounds too loud, too rough, too inhuman to be reassuring. Maybe she didn't recognize my voice. Or maybe she did, and she could recognize in my eyes a former classmate now cut off from her and everyone else in the world by stoneflesh.

She screamed, her face turning an angry red before she buried it in Mr. Remarkable's chest. She shrieked until she passed out.

He hypnotized her so she couldn't remember seeing me at all that day but would only remember a nice chat with Mr. Remarkable in which she gave him a good clue to understanding Count Zorndorf's escape whenever she would think about her visit to the Remarkable Building.

Me, I never tried to contact anyone else who knew Frank Melnik ever again. I threw myself into the battles against Zhulknor, the Shatterer and Kavallan (Team Remarkable # 82, # 85-6 and # 88-90). The fan mail poured in, and after that first year, I got my own book.

It sells pretty well. Boys buy it for the fights, and some girls buy it to look at Johnny Blast. At least that's what you tell me, Sam. Hey, as long as you make me look good, keep the stories light, and focus on zipping out to Moscow, Cairo or Antarctica to stop the Screaming Six from wrecking everything we hold dear, I'm happy.

Oh, geeze, Sam, it looks like I've almost filled this whole side of the tape just with your first question. Did I even answer it? What was it again?

How has becoming a superhero changed my life?

Oh, just say that I get fan mail, I've met some interesting people, and I don't have to wait for a table in a restaurant anymore.

The Red Lady

Sure I know about the Red Lady of Barclay Hall.

She doesn't exist. I know because I made her up.

You have no idea how boring graduate school can be. You grade scores of papers and exams by freshmen who don't know the difference between Abraham Lincoln and Julius Caesar, at the same time attending classes and seminars and doing your own research on how the American media covered Yugoslavia between 1945 and 1957 while you live on cafeteria food.

You can get a little slap-happy.

When you have a cube mate like Simpson, that happens sooner rather than later.

The first time I realized there was something wrong with Simpson was the first Thursday of the semester. A thunderstorm came up that morning, and Simpson showed up in Barclay 568 looking like a drowned kitten.

"Don't you have an umbrella?" I asked him.

"Channel 9 said it wouldn't rain today," he said.

That was Simpson. If somebody said it on TV, or, better yet, it was printed somewhere, it had to be true.

He was in American history writing about William Jennings Bryan. Simpson could recite the "Cross of Gold" speech at the drop of a hat, and he sincerely believed that railroad barons were the source of all evil in the world.

The fact that he was my cube mate proved that someone in the Department had a sadistic sense of humor.

I threw myself into my work, tried to avoid him, and, when I couldn't, took care to answer him in monosyllables.

Our cube was one of five in "the Loft," Room 568 in Barclay Hall. From the outside, Barclay Hall was a neat old building, a Gothic revival kind of thing. On the other hand, if you had to climb those five flights of stairs several times a day carrying your books and research, you soon realized there was more to life than architectural beauty.

"The Loft," as the Department called it, was the top floor of Barclay. We grad students called it "The Leper Colony." For some reason, the ceilings were shorter here than on the other floors. You always felt a little confined, a little "pressed-down" while you were up in the Leper Colony. The woodwork had darkened, and the lights seemed dimmer up here too.

One night in finals week, I stood by the window on the upper landing, watching the snow fall, and decided that Barclay Hall needed a ghost. Surely a place that looked like it escaped from the imagination of Charles Addams had to be haunted by more than the broken dreams of freshmen who weren't entirely sure when the War of 1812 happened.

What kind of ghost? It had to be female. Look, when you're a history grad student, a ghost is the only kind of female who will bother with you.

"Is everything okay?" Simpson asked me. "Are we going to get snowed out? They said on Channel 9 that we might get snowed out."

"I hope we don't," I said. "If the college gets snowed out, we get snowed in. With the ghost."

"What ghost?" Simpson asked.

"I shouldn't say," I said.

"Is there a ghost in Barclay Hall?"

Simpson grabbed my arm.

"Is there a ghost, Pete?"

I gave him a deeply significant look.

"That's not what Dr. Adkins wants us to believe," I said.

"Like in Jaws," Simpson said. "They didn't want people to know about the shark."

"Right," I said. "And Dr. Adkins doesn't want us to know about the ghost."

Simpson got right next to me.

"You know," he said, "I've never felt right on the fifth floor. When I'm up here, I always feel like something's pressing me down."

Instead of saying 'That's because the ceilings are goofy' I said:

"Have you ever seen the Red Lady?"

His eyes got wide. "Is that the ghost?"

I leaned in closer. "They say she killed herself. This used to be her house. The family money came from railroads, you know."

Simpson nodded eagerly.

"She was a real spoiled heiress," I said. "One year she wore a red dress to the Easter Ball. Everybody shunned her because of that, and she came home and killed herself. That's why she haunts the place."

How did I make that up? My grandmother always insisted on watching this Bette Davis movie about this woman who wears red to a ball, and everybody acts like it's a crime, and she finally dies. That was my inspiration for the Red Lady.

If Simpson had been anybody else, he would have laughed in my face.

Instead, he ate it all up.

He nodded at me. "I think I heard something like that once," he said. "The woman who died because she wore a red dress."

I should have laughed in his face then and ended it, but instead I just went back to the Leper Colony and graded another forty essay questions on why the French Revolution had gone wrong.

Going down the stairs that night, I met Thompson coming up. He was in economic history, something to do with how railroads replaced canals or some other topic that he found way more interesting than I did. Anyway, he smirked when he saw me.

"You told Simpson we've got a ghost?" he asked.

"Uh, yeah," I said.

"Cool," he said, his smirk getting bigger.

I filled him in on the Red Lady, and he walked away chuckling.

Telling Thompson was a mistake. Simpson got on my nerves, but he really got under Thompson's skin. That whole 'railroads are evil' thing, you know.

Anyway, I didn't think much about it. I went home for Christmas. When I came back to the cube I shared with Simpson, the photo of a stern young woman, her hair pulled up in a bun, with a cameo brooch at her throat, looked up at me from an old piece of newspaper on the desk.

THE LATE JESSICA BARCLAY, I read.

"What's this?" I asked.

Thompson hurried over.

"Pretty good, isn't it?" he asked.

He grinned as I looked at him.

"My brother's in L. A. So I'm out there, being a tourist, and I see Knott's Berry Farm. And they had this thing that let you make a Wild West newspaper, so I got this."

"Jessica Barclay?" I asked.

Thompson looked at me like I was stupid.

"The Red Lady of Barclay Hall," he said. "The one who wore scarlet to the ball, scandalized her beau, and came home and hanged herself in this very building." He tapped the photo. "There she is."

"How much did this set you back?" I asked.

"The look on Simpson's face was worth every penny."

"He's seen it?"

Thompson laughed.

"Seen it and swallowed it. He went to talk to Dr. Adkins about getting out of the Leper Colony."

I thought about that. Losing Simpson as a cube mate would be a pretty okay development.

Of course, Dr. Adkins could not be budged by a mere grad student. Simpson stayed in my cube, practically glued to my side, because he would not set foot in Barclay 568 unless I was there. I wasn't entirely sure how I was to protect him against the Red Lady, but apparently I was a guarantee against evil spectres.

The Red Lady didn't scare me. Simpson did. He really believed. Freshmen would come to him to complain about their grades, and he would tell each and every one about poor Jessica, the Red Lady of Barclay Hall and how her father never loved her and kept her away from boys her own age.

Where he got this stuff from, I have no idea. Probably from an old movie I never saw, thank God. I knew for a fact that Jessica had never lived, but after a few weeks, Simpson had me half convinced that she had walked weeping beneath these low ceilings for many years, looking out the windows for suitors who never came.

Simpson believed, and, as I watched those freshmen, I knew they believed too. The ones away from home for the first time, homesick, they sat there with their eyes getting bigger and bigger as Simpson told of Jessica's loneliness and agony, and I could see belief sprout.

Everyone who came through the door of Barclay 568 got an earful of the Red Lady from Simpson, and they told everybody. Their friends, classmates, people they knew from high school who went to other colleges, little siblings, anybody who looked interested, they all got the same word.

"My college has a ghost."

Who could resist that?

One Sunday in April, I had to finish a paper on the Trieste Crisis, so I spent the afternoon in the Cube. Simpson, thank God, had gone home for the weekend. I had the Leper Colony to myself, and I hammered out my paper. The afternoon slipped away, the light from the window had faded to purple, and I heard a whisper.

I sat very still in my chair.

"Is that where she hanged herself?" a female voice asked from the stairs.

"In that very room," another female said.

"Wow."

"It was this time of year," the second female said. "Easter. She came home in tears from the Easter Ball and went right to her room and hanged herself."

I rolled my eyes.

I made this stupid story up, I thought, *and I'm stopping it right now.*

I put my hands on the desk, and I shoved myself back. My chair's legs scraped across the floor, caught on something, and I tipped over, crashing to the floor.

"It's her!"

"We've heard the Red Lady!"

I moaned and heard feet thundering down the stairs.

"Oh, Jessica Barclay," I said as I looked up at the ceiling. "I hate you."

That was more years ago than I care to remember. I certainly couldn't take a fall like that so easily today. If you look at Youtube, you can see candlelight vigils of students in Barclay Hall in their red dresses. The University denies there is a ghost, but they don't discourage the vigils, and it seems that the Red Lady of Barclay Hall does attract a certain type of "creative" student and has boosted the profile of the University in the past few decades.

But take it from me, the Red Lady of Barclay Hall doesn't exist.

I should know. I made her up.

And I still hate her.

Acknowledgements

"The Dragon Lover" was published in The Fifth Di in 1994.

"Snowman" won First Place in the Lonesome Pine Short Story Contest in 2000. It was published in Lost State Voices III, the 2010 anthology of the Lost State Writers Guild.

"Kiss" was published in Lost State Voices, the 2005 anthology of the Lost State Writers Guild.

"After You Come Others" was published in the May 2005 issue of The Dogtown Review.

"Ol' Stoneface Speaks" was originally published in the Fall, 2012 issue of Jimson Weed, the literary magazine of University of Virginia's College at Wise.

"The Red Lady" won Second Place in the 2017 Lonesome Pine Short Story Contest.

I would like to thank the long-serving members of the Big Stone Gap Writers Group, Wendy Welch, Jenny Mullins, and James

Ryan, who read and commented on "A Regular Day – No Peanuts" and "Ol' Stoneface Speaks."

Also I'd like to thank Linda Campany and Delilah O'Haynes who heard some of these stories at the Abingdon Arts Depot years ago.

Rita Oakes, whom I met at TNEO 2001, very generously gave me useful comments on these stories as I organized this collection.

Special thanks to my wife Elizabeth, and my daughter Olivia and son Ethan, who put up with me as I wrote these stories.

Made in the USA
Middletown, DE
02 November 2019